Also by Michael Thomas Ford

SUICIDE NOTES

Z

Z

MICHAEL THOMAS FORD

HARPER TEEN

An Imprint of HarperCollinsPublishers

HarperTeen is an imprint of HarperCollins Publishers.

Z

Copyright © 2010 by Michael Thomas Ford
For information address HarperCollins Children's Books,
a division of HarperCollins Publishers, 10 East 53rd Street,
New York, NY 10022.
www.harperteen.com

Library of Congress Cataloging-in-Publication Data
Ford, Michael Thomas.
Z / Michael Thomas Ford. — 1st ed.
p. cm.
Summary: In the year 2032, after a virus that turned people
into zombies has been eradicated, Josh is invited to join an
underground gaming society where the gamers hunt zombies
and the action is more dangerous than it seems.
ISBN 978-0-06-073758-0
[1. Science fiction. 2. Role playing—Fiction. 3. Games—Fiction.
4. Zombies—Fiction.] I. Title.
PZ7.F7532119Zab 2010   2009044005
[Fic]—dc22   CIP
                                                        AC

Typography by Alison Klapthor
10 11 12 13 14   CG/RRDB   10 9 8 7 6 5 4 3 2 1
❖
First Edition

For Horrible Spider, Ocho Patas, and the Mungos,

who kept me company

For Kermit, Lorien, Delia Rose, and the friends
who saw me through

I

The zombie was somewhere ahead of him. Its stench—a combination of blood, dirt, and rotting meat—filled the air. It was close. Josh flipped the safety on his flamethrower and held it out in front of him, his finger on the trigger. Almost all the overhead lights were out, and the halogen light mounted on the barrel of his flamethrower had broken during a run-in with a z on a lower floor. He could see only about six feet ahead of him through the gloom.

The hospital's hallway was littered with trash; broken glass, charred pieces of paper, and twisted medical instruments were strewn around the floor. Dark smears streaked the white tile walls. Ahead of Josh a teddy bear sat propped against the wall just outside a partially open door, its fur stained with something black and sticky. Its head was torn off and lay in its lap. Stuffing puffed from the ragged neck.

Something about the bear caused a shiver to run down Josh's spine. Clearly it had belonged to a little kid. But where was the kid now? He hoped wherever it was, it hadn't already been turned by the zombies. Child zombies were the worst. Josh hated torching them.

But I will if I have to, he thought as he approached the door.

Using the end of his weapon, he nudged the door open. The only light in the room came from one ceiling fixture, and the bulb flickered as it tried to draw electricity from the hospital's ancient wiring. The room was visible for only a few seconds at a time as the light flashed on and off. Josh felt like he was watching an old movie being played on a broken projector.

Even with the limited light he could see enough to know that the woman on the bed was dead. She was dressed in a nurse's uniform, her white dress stained with what could only be blood. Her head lolled to one side so that her face was turned toward Josh. Her eyes were gone, and there was a ragged hole in her throat where the zombie had bitten her. One arm was stretched out, and the fingers of that hand were curled, clutching a clump of long blond hair that was attached to a piece of bloody scalp. On the floor below the hand, a hypodermic needle lay in a pool of liquid.

She tried to kill it with the needle, Josh thought. *But it got her.*

Part of him was glad she was dead. If she'd been alive, he would have had to torch her, since she'd obviously been bitten and therefore could infect other people. That was the First Rule of Torching: Cleanse with fire.

Suddenly something scrambled out from under the bed, heading for the far side of the room. Whatever it was whimpered like a frightened animal. Instinctively Josh raised his flamethrower. But the thing was running *away* from him. If it had been a zombie, it would have come at him. They never ran away. He took his finger off the flamethrower's trigger.

"Are you okay?" he called out. He was thinking about the teddy bear. Had the child who owned it been in the room when the zombie attacked? Maybe the kid had hidden under the bed and escaped the zombie's notice. If so, it was Josh's responsibility to help. That was the Second Rule of Torching: Save all humans.

When the light flickered back on for a moment, he searched the shadows. Huddled in the corner of the room was a little girl. Maybe six or seven years old, she was wearing a torn, dirty dress and no shoes. Her long hair hung down in her face. She was breathing quickly, and as Josh approached, she pressed herself against the wall and began shaking her head from side to side.

"No," she said softly. "Don't kill me. Please."

Josh stopped and crouched down. "It's okay," he said. "I'm not going to hurt you. What's your name?"

The little girl stared at him. He searched her eyes for any sign of the infection, but in the dim light he couldn't see well enough to tell for sure. She *seemed* okay.

That kind of thinking can get you killed, he told himself. But he had to help. He couldn't just leave the girl there.

"Vi—" the girl said. Her voice cracked when she spoke, and she tried again. "Vi . . . Violet."

"Hi, Violet. I'm Josh. You and I are going to get out of here, okay?"

"But the monsters . . ." Violet said. She looked at the body on the bed, and her mouth began to tremble.

"Look at me," Josh told her. "Violet, look at me."

When the girl was looking at him, he held out his hand to her. "It's going to be okay."

Violet hesitated a moment, then took his hand. He helped her to her feet. He could feel her shaking. *I don't blame her,* he thought. He wanted to ask how she'd survived so long in the hospital without a zombie finding her, but now was not the time.

"We're going to go into the hall now," he told Violet.

She pulled away, shaking her head. "They're out there," she said. "They're waiting for us."

"Most of them are dead," said Josh. "My friend and I took care of them."

"Where is your friend now?" Violet asked.

You shouldn't have said anything, you idiot. Josh scolded himself for his mistake. The fact was, he didn't know whether Firecracker was alive or dead. His com-link had broken during the scuffle with the zombie in the operating room on the fourth floor, and he hadn't been able to reach him since. All he got was static. He hoped his buddy wasn't dead—or, even worse, turned. Then he would have to torch him too. *The Third Rule of Torching,* he thought. *You can't bring them back.*

He pushed the thought from his mind and focused on Violet. He needed her to listen to him, otherwise both of them could end up as zombie food. "We'll meet up with my friend soon," he said, hoping that was true. "Right now you just have to trust me, okay?"

Violet looked into his eyes. Her own were barely visible in the still-blinking light. "Okay," she said softly.

Josh led Violet from the room, making sure to

keep himself between her and the bed so that she wouldn't have to look at the dead nurse. He noticed that the little girl kept her head down until they were in the hallway. *Smart kid.* "We're going to go to the end of this hallway," he said. "There's an elevator there, and we're going to take it down to the first floor and get out of here."

"Is everybody dead?" Violet asked. "The nurses? The doctors? All the people?"

"Just stay behind me," said Josh, ignoring her question.

As they reached each new doorway, Josh peered inside, always keeping his finger on the trigger of his flamethrower. But the rooms were all empty. Whoever had been in them was either eaten or turned.

Finally they came to the end of the hall. In front of them were the elevator doors. Hallways continued both to the left and to the right. Josh made a quick scan, saw nothing, and hit the down button on the elevator's control panel. He hoped the hospital's unreliable wiring would hold up long enough for them to get out. Somewhere below them came the sound of machinery grinding to life, then the *thuck-thuck-thuck* as the elevator car rose up on its heavy cable.

As the hand on the dial above the elevator doors slowly crept from *B* to *1* to *2*, Josh surveyed the hallways in each direction. If there were any zombies on the floor, they would have heard the elevator and started to move toward the sound. *Good thing they're slow*, he thought. Still, they could move when they needed to. He knew that from experience. And all it took was one bite to ruin your day.

The 3 on the dial lit up. "Come on," Josh urged the clanking machinery. "Hurry up."

As the dial hit 4 and moved past it to 5—the floor they were on—Josh felt himself relax a little bit. They were almost there. Now he just had to hope the elevator didn't have any riders in it.

"Stand back," he told Violet, moving away from the elevator doors just in case he had to put the burn on anything inside.

Violet obeyed. Then, as the door began to open, Josh heard her call out, "Dr. Rackham!"

Josh whirled around in time to see the girl dashing down the left-hand corridor toward the figure of a man in a long white coat. He carried a clipboard in one hand, and there was a stethoscope around his neck.

"Dr. Rackham!" Violet yelled. "Come with us! We're getting out!"

The clipboard fell from the doctor's hand as he suddenly lurched sideways. At that moment the overhead light came on, and the man's face was bathed in harsh fluorescent light. The blood on his cheeks was bright red—fresh—and a scalpel extended from one of his eyes, plunged through a cracked lens of his glasses.

Violet stopped, staring at the lumbering figure. The zombie reached out toward her and moaned. Blood and something darker oozed from his lips in thick strings.

"Violet!" Josh yelled. "Get down!"

The little girl looked back at him. The zombie doctor was only a dozen feet from her. If she didn't act immediately, the doctor would reach her in a matter of seconds.

"Violet, NOW!" Josh yelled.

Violet fell to the floor, lying on her stomach and covering her head with her arms. Josh aimed his gun at the zombie and pulled the trigger. A column of flame erupted from the muzzle and flew toward the doctor. His lab coat caught most of it and burst into tongues of orange and yellow that licked hungrily at the material. The zombie looked down at himself and pawed uselessly at the flames.

Josh fired another round at the creature, this time aiming for its face. The zombie's skin crackled and burst open, and the doctor swayed from side to side. One of his hands was on fire, and he waved it around like a grotesque torch.

"Violet! Come on!" Josh shouted.

The girl raised herself up and ran to him. Not once did she look back at the zombie, who had fallen to the floor and was now fully consumed in fire. Black smoke poured from him and the smell of burning flesh was thick in the air.

The elevator doors opened just as Violet reached Josh. The box held no surprise visitors, and Josh pushed Violet inside and followed after her. He hit the button for the ground floor and watched as the heavy doors slid shut. The elevator began to descend.

Violet was crying. She was crouched in the corner, her arms around her knees, breathing in jagged gasps. Josh knelt down, but when he reached out to comfort her, she recoiled.

"It's okay now," Josh told her. "We're almost out of here."

Violet rested her forehead on her knees and rocked back and forth. Josh glanced at the panel on the wall. They were passing the third floor. *Why is it taking so long?* he wondered, willing the elevator to move faster.

As the second-floor button lit up there was a heavy *thud* on the car's roof. The whole box shook. Violet screamed as the escape hatch in the elevator's ceiling opened and a face looked down into the car. The skin was peeled away on one side, exposing muscle and bone. The eyes were clouded over with a milky yellow film, and the creature's torn lips grinned horribly.

Josh felt as if he'd been punched in the stomach. "Firecracker," he whispered, his voice cracking as he recognized his friend even through the damage that had been done to his face.

But he's not your friend anymore, he reminded himself. *He's a meatbag.*

Instinctively he raised his flamethrower then stopped as he realized that he would just end up spraying the inside of the box with fire. He might destroy the zombie, but the elevator would become an oven, and he and Violet would be cooked alive. Instead he tried to shut the hatch with the end of his gun. But the zombie threw himself forward and tumbled down on top of Josh, pinning him to the ground.

Josh looked into what was left of Firecracker's face. There was nothing of his friend there—just a monster that was coming toward him with his mouth open, ready to bite. Josh raised his arm to protect himself, but he knew that even one bite that broke the skin would mean the end for him.

"Get off him!"

Violet's voice broke through the silence. Firecracker paused. Turning his head, he looked at the little girl. It was the break Josh needed. Putting a hand on Firecracker's chest, he shoved as hard as he could, and Firecracker rolled onto his back.

As Josh scrambled to his feet, the elevator shuddered to a stop and the doors opened. Josh grabbed Violet's hand. He looked for his gun, but it was trapped beneath Firecracker, who had rolled onto his knees and was trying to get to his feet. There was no way Josh could get the flamethrower.

"Run!" Josh ordered. "Run down the hall and out the front door. You'll be safe there."

Violet didn't move. She stood in the doorway, staring into the flickering half-light of the hallway. At the other end of the hall, the doors to the hospital glowed faintly as sunlight penetrated the grimy glass.

"Go!" Josh yelled, pushing Violet out of the elevator.

The girl ran. Josh turned back to Firecracker, who was on his feet and moving his head from side to side as if he couldn't see. The flamethrower was on the floor behind him. Josh considered his choices—he could leave his gun and follow Violet out of the hospital. But that would leave Firecracker in there, where he would still be able to infect anyone foolish enough to venture inside the building. He couldn't let that happen. Plus, Josh couldn't stand to see his friend the way he was. He knew Firecracker would want to be put out of his misery, even if he was no longer human and didn't know what he'd become. Josh would want the same thing if he were in Firecracker's place.

He made his decision. He dived for the gun, reaching between Firecracker's legs and grabbing the flamethrower by the barrel. Moving more quickly than he thought possible, he scrambled back out of the elevator and got to his feet. The gun in his hands was now pointed at Firecracker.

"I'm sorry, buddy," Josh said as he raised the flamethrower and released the safety. A tiny blue flame flickered at the head of the barrel. Josh squeezed the trigger.

"Hey!" a shrill voice yelled. "It's time for dinner. Mom says to get your butt downstairs now."

Josh whirled around. His sister Emily stood in the doorway to his room. Her hands were on her hips and her blond hair was tied in pigtails. She looked past him at the computer screen, and her eyes lit up.

"Busted!" she said triumphantly. "I am *so* telling Mom and Dad."

Josh tore the virtual-reality helmet from his head and tried to turn off the computer. As he did, he heard a robotic voice say, "Mission failed. You will turn in five, four, three—"

Glancing at the screen, Josh saw his avatar on the

floor just outside the elevator. Firecracker was kneeling beside him, gnawing on his neck. Blood pooled around his body.

"Two, one," the voice concluded as Josh finally managed to turn the screen off. He knew what happened next, and he didn't want to see it.

"Damn!" Josh exclaimed. He turned to his sister. "Look what you made me do."

"They're going to ground you for forever," Emily crowed. "You know what they said *last* time they caught you playing that game."

Of course he knew. His parents had been furious, especially his mother. She'd grounded him for two whole weeks and threatened to take away his computer privileges for another two. Only after he'd apologized repeatedly and promised not to play anymore had she relented.

He'd kept his word for three days. Then the lure of the game had proved too strong, and one night he found himself logging in. Since then he'd played secretly, always careful to lock his door when he was gaming. For some reason, this time he'd forgotten to, and Emily had caught him.

Josh wanted to yell at his sister some more, but he knew that would only make things worse. Emily had him in a corner.

"I'll make you a deal," he said.

Emily crossed her arms over her chest and cocked her head. "What kind of deal?" she asked.

Although he was angry, Josh had to stifle a laugh. For a nine-year-old his sister was a tough negotiator. Just a week before, she'd managed to get their parents to up her allowance by two dollars a week by arguing that since her eighth birthday the rate of inflation had increased by 7 percent while her allowance had increased by only 5 percent.

"I'll do half your chores for a month," he suggested.

Emily shook her head. "Uh-uh," she said. "Mom would wonder why you're doing the dishes. Try again."

Josh groaned. He didn't have much else to bargain with. Then he thought of something. "I'll give you issues one through twelve of *Changeling Quest*."

He saw Emily hesitate. *Changeling Quest* was her favorite graphic novel series, but she had started reading it at issue thirteen and didn't own the first dozen. They were no longer available for download, and only people who had purchased unlocking codes could access them on their Cybook readers. As with all Cybooks, the codes could be transferred one time to a new reader, and sometimes they showed up for sale on used Cybook sites, but it would have cost Emily a year's allowance to get her own set.

She was always asking Josh if she could borrow his reader to read the novels, and he knew how badly she wanted to own them herself. He didn't particularly like the series, but he had held on to the codes in case Emily ever had something he wanted to trade for. Now she did. He just had to pretend that giving them up was a big deal.

"Come on," he said. "It's all I've got. And you know you want to have them." He tried to sound sad about possibly losing the Cybooks.

"Issues one through twelve *and* your Spider Queen action figure," Emily countered.

"No way!" Josh said, now genuinely upset. "I saved up for that for six months. They only made two hundred of them, and mine's number twenty-two. And it's not an action figure. It's a handmade, one-twenty-eighth-scale *articulated model*."

Emily turned around. "Hey, Mom!" she called out.

"Wait!" Josh said.

Emily looked at him. "Deal?" she asked.

"I'll give you the novels and do your homework for *two* months."

Emily rolled her eyes. "Please," she said. "I want to get *good* grades. Mom!" she yelled again. "Josh is—"

"Okay!" Josh cut her off. "You can have the Cybooks and the Spider Queen. It's a deal."

Emily looked at him, beaming. "Transfer the codes," she said.

Josh shook his head. "Not until after dinner," he said. "I want to make sure you don't squeal."

"Like I would go back on a deal," Emily said, sounding offended.

Josh knew she was right. Emily drove a hard bargain, but she always did what she agreed to. Still, he couldn't let her win so easily. He stared back, saying nothing.

"Fine," Emily relented. "But *right after* dinner."

She left the room. Josh turned his computer screen back on and saw the message he'd been dreading: YOU HAVE BEEN DEMOTED ONE LEVEL. REPORT TO THE BRIEFING ROOM FOR YOUR NEXT ASSIGNMENT.

"One level!" Josh groaned. After almost a year of playing, he had recently reached Torcher First Class. Now he was back to being a Torcher Second Class. It would take months to get his rank back. His only consolation was that Firecracker would also be demoted for getting turned. Still, it didn't make him feel any better.

"Great," he said as he got up to go downstairs. "Back to the minor leagues."

2

"**Y**ou gave her what?" Firecracker looked at Josh as if his friend had completely lost his mind. They were sitting in biology class, waiting for the late bell to ring.

"I had to," Josh objected. "She was going to tell my folks, and you know how they feel about the game. If they knew I was playing again, they'd put a block on my computer so all I could access is educational sites. No more gaming. At all."

Firecracker ran a hand through his red hair. "I guess you kinda deserve it," he said. "You did almost torch me."

"That's my *job*," Josh reminded him. "Besides, no one told you to go and get bit. What happened, anyway?"

Firecracker shook his head. "Man, it was Charlie again. He tricked me into following him down to the morgue. When I got there, he was hiding inside one of the meat freezers so I couldn't smell him. Jumped out from behind a side of beef that was hanging in there and got me."

"That guy is *good*," said Josh. "What level is he now, thirty-six or something?"

"I don't even know," Firecracker answered. "Whatever he is, he's the best player I've ever seen."

"Too bad he plays a z," said Josh.

"Yeah," Firecracker agreed. "I don't get that. Why would he want to play a meatbag?" He spoke the last word as if he were spitting something nasty-tasting out of his mouth.

Josh shrugged. He didn't understand it either. Most players wanted to be Torchers. But Charlie played the other side. He'd started playing only a few months before Josh and Firecracker did, but quickly shot up the rankings and was now one of the top zombie players. Even Josh had to admit that playing a z was more difficult than playing a Torcher. You had to be really good at tricking the other players and leading them into traps where you could bite them. And Charlie was a master of it. Yet no one knew much about him. *I'd sure like to meet him,* thought Josh as Mrs. Hotchkiss entered the room.

"All right," said Mrs. Hotchkiss. "Let's get started."

She punched a button on the control panel on her desk, and the lights in the room dimmed. A moment later a three-dimensional holographic image of a brain appeared in the air in front of each desk. It rotated slowly, giving the students a view of all sides.

"The human brain is a complex organ," the teacher said. "But, according to the triune brain theory first proposed by neurologist Paul MacLean way back in the 1950s, it comprises three basic sections."

She typed on her keypad, and one section of the brain—the largest—turned blue. "This is the neocortex," she explained. "This part of the brain is responsible for things such as language development, abstract thought, and consciousness."

She continued on to the second section, which was within the brain, surrounded by the neocortex. "This is the limbic system," she explained as the area turned yellow. "It's responsible for memory storage and emotions."

The hologram of the brain had been transferred to Josh's NoteTaker unit, and as Mrs. Hotchkiss spoke, the information was updated on his screen. Since Josh could always look at it later, he didn't listen too closely.

The final area, an oddly shaped section deep within the brain, turned green. It reminded Josh of a flower on a stalk.

"And this," Mrs. Hotchkiss said, "is the most primitive part of the brain. It's called the R-complex or, more commonly, the reptilian brain."

"As in lizards?" Marcus Pell asked, earning him laughs from his classmates.

"Actually, yes," the teacher confirmed. "In reptiles the R-complex makes up almost all of the brain, controlling basic functions such as body temperature, heart rate, and breathing. It does the same for us, although thanks to the other parts of our brains, most of us are slightly more advanced than lizards."

Again most of the class laughed. Josh, however, drew on the page of his NoteTaker, using the stylus to make a series of spirals. Biology was one of his least favorite classes. As far as he was concerned, it was interesting only when they were dissecting holofrogs or doing cloning experiments. Plus, Mrs. Hotchkiss's voice always made him sleepy.

"I bring this up because I understand you're studying the zombie war in Mr. Sumpana's history class," said his teacher. "Do any of you know the science behind zombiism?"

Josh was suddenly interested. No one raised a hand, but he could see that the whole class was paying attention. Even Firecracker, in the row ahead of Josh, was sitting up and listening.

"Most of you probably know that the zombie epidemic began with a new strain of the common flu virus," Mrs. Hotchkiss said. Her fingers moved over her keypad, and a small red image appeared beside the brain. It was circular, with hundreds of tiny bumps on it. It spun slowly.

"We've all had the flu at one time or another," the teacher said. "You know the symptoms: sneezing, fever, feeling tired. The zombie flu was the same. That's why at first nobody knew how dangerous it was. With the first cases, it took several weeks for the more severe symptoms to appear, and by then it was too late."

Suddenly the holographic virus penetrated the smallest area of the brain, which began to glow red. As Josh watched, the reptilian portion of the brain grew in size while the other two sections shrank.

"The zombie virus attacked the reptilian brain," explained Mrs. Hotchkiss, "making it grow larger. At the same time, it caused the other two brain areas to shrink. As the reptilian brain took over control of the body, the infected person lost the ability to think rationally and to make judgments based on right and wrong. Instead infected people began to act more and more impulsively, until eventually the only things that were important to them were eating and survival."

A girl in the front row raised her hand. "I thought zombies were the living dead," she said.

"Yes and no," Mrs. Hotchkiss answered. "As the zombie flu virus attacked the neocortex of the brain, infected people lost the ability to speak coherently. In addition, they developed a great tolerance for pain. They seemed not to be affected by injuries that would be devastating to you and me."

"You mean they couldn't be killed?" someone asked.

"Not easily," said Mrs. Hotchkiss. "In addition to affecting the brain, the virus had a peculiar effect on the blood. It became thicker and coagulated more easily. Wounds didn't bleed as much, so a zombie could be stabbed or shot and survive. Some even lost limbs but didn't bleed to death as we would, because their blood clotted so quickly. Because of this, it was first assumed that the virus killed the infected person and then somehow reanimated the corpse. In reality, those infected with the zombie flu did not die first. They simply became zombies because their brains were attacked by the virus, and it destroyed the most human parts and let the primitive part take over."

"But you just said 'yes and no,'" Josh reminded her.

"They were alive in the sense that they breathed and moved and had heartbeats," the teacher said.

"But their memories and emotions were gone. Their ability to feel was destroyed. They didn't think in any way we would consider human. But technically, yes, they were alive."

"Why didn't they just give them a shot or something?" Josh was surprised to hear Firecracker ask the question. He almost never spoke in class.

"That's a good question," Mrs. Hotchkiss answered. "Doctors didn't give them a vaccine because they didn't have one. The flu virus is a very simple one, but that's also what makes it difficult to fight. It mutates very rapidly when it's attacked, which means that what works for one form of the virus might not work for another. In the case of zombie flu, none of the vaccines they tried worked, at least not quickly enough to save those who were already infected."

"But we get zombie flu shots now," said Josh. "When we're born. So they came up with something, right?"

Mrs. Hotchkiss nodded. "There's a preventative vaccine now," she said. "It's based on the most common strain of the zombie flu virus."

"But there could be other kinds, couldn't there?" asked Firecracker.

"Theoretically, yes," said the teacher. "However, there hasn't been a documented case of zombie flu infection in over fifteen years. The possibility of a new strain finding its way into the general population is almost nonexistent. In other words, Mr. McPherson, you don't have to worry about turning into a zombie anytime soon."

Firecracker grinned. "Too bad," he said. "It sounds like fun."

The class laughed, but Mrs. Hotchkiss shook her head. "It was *not* fun, Mr. McPherson," she said, her voice serious. "None of you have seen a real zombie. But I have. Most people my age have. Your parents probably have. Those who were infected with the virus suffered horribly. The only consolation for those of us who saw them suffer was that by the time they turned, they had stopped being human. They didn't know what they were."

"Why did they torch them?"

Josh's attention was brought back to the class by the question. It had come from Elizabeth Stalin, who sat right behind him.

Mrs. Hotchkiss hesitated a moment. "The zombie flu virus was initially passed on through saliva," she said. "A zombie would bite someone, and the virus would enter the person's bloodstream. Once it was in the blood, the virus could then be passed on through that. If someone had an open cut—or any kind of wound that exposed the body to potential infection—coming into contact with zombie blood was dangerous. It was feared that the virus might become airborne next, which would have been disastrous. So it was decided that the least risky and most efficient way to destroy the virus was to burn the zombies."

"But wouldn't that really hurt?" someone asked.

Again Mrs. Hotchkiss took some time before answering. "By that point the infected people were functioning solely on primitive reactions," she said. "Almost like puppets being controlled by strings that were being pulled by their reptilian brains. They most likely didn't know what was happening."

"Still, it must have hurt," Elizabeth insisted. "They still had nerves and stuff."

Firecracker turned around and looked at her. "Who cares?" he said. "They were *meatbags*, not people."

"Yeah," said another girl. "Besides, if people hadn't burned the zombies, they would have turned a lot of other people into zombies."

"The important thing is that we don't have to worry about it anymore," Mrs. Hotchkiss said. "As I said earlier, there hasn't been a documented case since before you were born."

Josh raised his hand. "Where did it come from?" he asked. "The virus, I mean."

"Nobody really knows," his teacher told him. "Most likely it was simply a very strong mutation. As you've seen, there was nothing supernatural about zombies. They were just people who got sick and essentially devolved into primitive life forms."

"My uncle says the Russians did it," Firecracker announced. "He says they wanted to wipe us out."

"Then they didn't do a very good job," said Mrs. Hotchkiss. "Just as many people turned in Russia as did here. I think your uncle has been watching a little too much television."

"He was a Torcher," Firecracker said defensively. "He should know."

"Yes," said Mrs. Hotchkiss. "Well, I'm sure we're all very thankful to him for his service. Now if you'll access sequence 1872-A, this will show you how the zombie flu virus interrupted the messages sent from one part of the brain to the others. This is going to be on your test on Friday, so let's go over it and see if there's anything you don't understand."

Josh keyed the number into his NoteTaker and looked at the diagram that appeared on the screen. He listened as his teacher went over the various parts, but mostly he was thinking about his aunt Lucy, his mother's sister. He'd never met her, but he'd seen pictures. She was really pretty, just like his mom.

And she had turned into a zombie.

She was only sixteen when she got sick, one of the first in the country to get the virus. He'd heard the story several times from his mother, but they didn't talk about it too much because it made his mother sad. And Josh didn't talk about it with anyone else. Not even Firecracker knew. Josh wasn't sure why he didn't tell anyone. He wasn't ashamed, exactly. Having a zombie in your family wasn't the terrible thing it had once been; it just wasn't something most people talked about.

I guess it doesn't really make it any better to know that she was just sick, he thought. It was amazing that something as tiny as a virus could turn someone into a monster like that. *But she probably didn't even know it was happening,* he told himself.

Mrs. Hotchkiss continued to talk about zombies, and for a change Josh listened to every word. When he heard the bell ring, he was actually disappointed that class was over. Reluctantly he gathered up his things and filed into the hallway along with everyone else. Firecracker caught up with him as he walked to his locker.

"You up for hunting reptile brains tonight?" he asked.

"You know I am," said Josh.

"Excellent," Firecracker said. "We've got some work to do if we want to get our rankings back." He punched Josh hard in the shoulder. "And this time, try not to screw up."

"Hey!" Josh protested. "You're the one who got—"

But Firecracker was already making his way upstairs to his next class.

"Bit!" Josh shouted after him. "*You* got bit!"

3

"**A**ll right, let's do this."

Josh spoke into the small microphone mounted inside his helmet as he prepared to play. He had already put on the interactive gloves that allowed him to move his character through the holographic landscape as if he were really there. When he looked through the lenses of his helmet, instead of his room he saw the front doors of the downtown public library building.

The creators of the game had mapped the entire city, and gamers could play in holographic recreations of every building, subway, and sewer. The zombie generator was random, so any place you went into could be infested with the creatures.

Josh leaned back in his chair and took a deep breath, allowing the sense stimulators in his helmet to kick in. They allowed him to feel, smell, and sometimes even taste things he came into contact with during the game. Of course some sensations—like zombie bites or the effects of torching—were blocked to prevent players from becoming overstimulated. Still, when those things happened in a game, the sounds and sights alone were enough to make a player imagine what it would feel like.

He knew he shouldn't be playing, but he couldn't resist. Torching was exciting. Hunting for z's and wiping them out made him feel like a real soldier. He loved the way he got more and more tense as he searched for the zombies, the way his senses became so intensely focused as he worried about staying alive and saving the other humans. He especially liked the adrenaline rush that came when he finally found the z's and torched them.

He looked to his right, where Firecracker stood checking the controls on his flamethrower. "Ready?" Josh asked.

"Let's torch some meatbags," Firecracker answered. He flipped the safety on his flamethrower, which erupted in a short burst of fire.

"Easy," Josh warned him. "We don't want to burn the place down."

Josh pushed open the huge door, which swung inward with a groan, and he and Firecracker stepped into the cavernous lobby of the library. The marble floor stretched away into the darkness, while the ceiling towered four floors above them. Books, most of them torn apart, were strewn everywhere. A thick smear of blood ran the length of the circulation desk, as if a body had been dragged along it.

Josh followed the trail to the end, and saw the body of a woman crumpled among a pile of books. Firecracker approached the woman, his flamethrower held out in front of him. When he was a dozen feet away from her, he turned back to Josh. "She's gone," he said. "Well, her head is, and she's not going anywhere without it."

"Just leave her there," Josh said. "We'll clean up on the way out."

Leaving the woman behind, he and Firecracker advanced deeper into the library. Josh listened for any sound of moaning or shuffling, but there was nothing. Then, all of a sudden, a figure burst from the shadows. Josh aimed his flamethrower at it, but a voice called out, "Don't shoot! I'm human!"

"Stand down!" Josh ordered Firecracker, who he could see was itching to set something on fire. Reluctantly Firecracker lowered his weapon.

The figure came closer, and Josh saw that it was a girl. She wasn't dressed in a Torcher uniform, which meant that she was part of the game, a character generated by the system itself. These characters made the game even more fun, but they could also make it more difficult, especially if they got in the way.

The girl was wearing a fluffy black fur jacket with a white hood. The hood had two small, round, black ears on it, and around the girl's eyes were large black circles. Josh looked down and saw that she was wearing white fur shorts and knee-high boots made out of black fur. *She's supposed to be a panda bear,* he thought.

"Great," said Firecracker. "A Zooey."

Zooeys were a problem. In real life they were people who liked to dress as animals. They listened to Japanese pop music and spent their time watching horror movies and eating candy. They were freaky but harmless, and Josh had no problem with the Zooeys generated by the game. In the game, though, they were unreliable. Sometimes they gave you good information, but sometimes they just made stuff up—stuff that would get you killed if you weren't careful.

"What are you doing here?" Josh asked the Zooey.

"Nothing," the girl said. She was breathing heavily and kept looking behind her.

"Nothing?" said Firecracker. "You mean you always run around the library playing hide-and-seek?"

"Okay," the girl admitted. "We wanted to see them for ourselves."

Firecracker groaned. "Of course you did," he said. "Stupid tourists."

"What's your name?" Josh asked.

He wasn't surprised when the girl answered, "Pandy."

"How many of you are there?"

"Just two," she said. "Me and Monkey. Oh, and Rabbit. I guess that's three."

Firecracker looked at Josh. "Please just let me torch her," he said.

"No," Josh answered. "We could lose points."

Pandy came closer, and Josh saw that there was blood on the fur of her jacket. He also saw that one hand was covered in a mitten that resembled a bear paw. The other mitten dangled from a string attached to Pandy's jacket. The nails on that hand were painted bubble-gum pink.

"We were downstairs," Pandy said. "In the children's section. Monkey was reading to us from *Alice in Wonderland*," she continued. "Then one of *them* came out of nowhere. It grabbed Monkey and it . . ." Her voice trailed off as she started to cry.

"Yeah, yeah," Firecracker said. "It bit her. We know the routine."

Pandy hiccuped as she tried to stop crying. "It all happened so fast," she sobbed.

"It's all right," Josh said. "We'll find your friends."

"What about me?" Pandy asked. "Don't leave me here."

"Go outside," Josh told her. "Wait on the front steps."

"But my friends!" Pandy wailed.

"We *said* we'll find them and take care of them," Firecracker reminded her. He flicked his flamethrower on, and Pandy's eyes grew wide.

"Go outside," Josh said again. "Now."

Pandy obeyed, running for the front door and disappearing outside. Josh checked his flamethrower to make sure it was on, then nodded for Firecracker to follow him.

"If I'd known we were going to be on a Zooey rescue mission, I would have picked the sewer assignment," Firecracker said.

"Humans are humans," Josh reminded him. "We get the same amount of credit whether we save a Zooey or the mayor."

"I know," said Firecracker. "But half the time they're just lying. It drives me nuts."

As they walked down the wide staircase that descended to the lower level, Josh looked for any signs of activity. Halfway down they came upon something that looked like a giant cotton ball. Josh bent down to look at it and saw that it was covered in blood.

"I'm guessing Rabbit didn't make it," Firecracker said.

"Looks that way," Josh agreed. "Be careful. I have a feeling we're close."

They reached the lower level. The children's section wasn't as large as the upstairs, but it was big enough that they couldn't see from one end to the other. The walls were papered with cheerful posters featuring favorite characters from children's books, and the reading tables and chairs were less than half the size of those in the rest of the library. Josh felt like a giant as he walked through the room.

Suddenly a high-pitched whistling sound broke the silence. Josh looked up and saw a zombie shuffling toward them. It was a woman wearing a blood-splattered dress and shaking a finger at them. The whistling sound came from a jagged hole in her throat.

As the zombie got closer, Josh saw that she was wearing a name tag: MRS. JARVIS, CHILDREN'S LIBRARIAN.

"A meatbag librarian?" Firecracker said, sounding disgusted.

Josh aimed at her with his flamethrower. "Sorry, Mrs. Jarvis," he said. "I'm afraid you're overdue."

"Josh!"

The noise made him jump. He ripped his helmet off and whirled around. "Emily, I thought we had a deal!" he yelled, expecting to see his sister standing behind him.

"Oh, really?" said his mother. "And what kind of deal would that be?"

Josh dropped the helmet and jumped up, trying to block the screen. "Mom," he said. "I was just—"

"I see what you were doing," she said. She walked over and turned the simulator off. The library disappeared.

"But Firecracker!" Josh protested. "And my points!"

"Josh, you know how we feel about that game," his mother said. "You were supposed to be doing homework."

"I was just playing for a few minutes," Josh argued. "I don't see why you make such a big deal about killing a few zom—"

He saw his mother's face grow pale. "I'm sorry," he said quickly. "I didn't mean to—"

"Sit down," she interrupted.

Josh sat in the chair at his desk. His mother

remained standing. "I really am sorry, Mom," Josh said.

"Just—just listen for a minute," his mother told him.

Josh nodded.

"I know that to you this is just a game," his mother said. "You're young. The war probably seems like ancient history. But for those of us who lived through it, it wasn't a game." Her voice caught.

"Aunt Lucy," said Josh, feeling horrible for hurting his mother's feelings.

His mother was quiet for a moment. When she looked at Josh, he saw sadness in her eyes. "She wasn't much older than you are now when she turned," she said. "I'll never forget coming home from school that day."

Josh didn't say anything. His mother had never shared the details of what had happened. He found himself both wanting to know and wishing she wouldn't tell him.

His mother continued. "We thought she just had the flu, so she'd stayed home for a few days. That day I'd gotten her homework assignments from her teachers so that she wouldn't get behind. When I went into the kitchen, there was a pot on the stove. My mother had been making chicken soup." She smiled. "She always made chicken soup when one of us didn't feel well," she said. "But it was boiling over, as if something had interrupted my mother while she was cooking."

She took a deep breath. "That's when I saw the blood," she told Josh. "It started in the doorway and went into the dining room. I remember following it and wondering what it could be. My brain didn't want to believe it was blood, even though I could smell it." She shook her head. "I'll never forget that smell, not as long as I live."

Josh almost told her to stop, but his mouth wouldn't work. His heart was beating more quickly, almost as if he were playing the game. He hated seeing his mother upset, but he wanted to hear the rest of the story.

"I followed the blood up the stairs to Lucy's room," said his mother. Her voice was shaky. She stopped speaking, and when she looked at Josh she seemed to be looking right through him at something only she could see. "My father was on the floor," she said. "One of his arms had been ripped off, and his head was turned so that it looked like he was staring at me, but he was dead. My mother was lying on the bed. Lucy was kneeling over her. Her face and her nightgown were covered in blood."

The room was completely silent as Josh waited for his mother to continue. She continued to look through him.

"What did you do?" Josh asked, his voice barely a whisper.

His mother shook her head. "I didn't do anything," she said. "Not for a long time. I told myself I was dreaming and that I would wake up and Lucy would be sitting peacefully in bed, eating chicken soup."

She blinked, and now she *was* looking at Josh. "Then Lucy saw me," she said, her voice harder. "She looked right at me, and when I saw her eyes, I knew my sister was gone. When she jumped off the bed and came at me, I ran to my room and shut the door. Lucy was screaming and grunting and clawing at the door like a rabid animal. I knew that if she got in, she would tear me apart. I had my cell phone, and I called 911 and told the operator that my sister had gone crazy. She stayed on the phone with me until the police got there."

"The police?" Josh said.

"The Torchers hadn't been established yet," his mother explained. "They weren't formed until things got worse. And when Lucy turned, we didn't know about the zombies yet. I really did think she'd just gone crazy. When the police got there, I heard them shouting as they came upstairs. Then I heard Lucy run at them howling. And then I heard the shots."

She closed her eyes as a tear slipped out. "A minute

or two later someone knocked on my door and asked if I was all right," she said. "I said I was, and unlocked the door. But they told me to lie down on the floor in the middle of the room, and when they came in they pointed their rifles at me until they could look at my eyes. Even then they took me to the hospital and kept me there for a week to see if I showed any symptoms of infection."

Josh didn't know what to say. He imagined his mother in the hospital, knowing that her entire family was dead, not knowing what she would do when she got out. She'd been younger than he was now. He didn't know if he could handle something like that. He tried to find a way to apologize to his mother, but everything he thought of sounded stupid.

"It wasn't just what happened to Lucy that was so terrifying," his mother said after a while. "I mean at first it was, of course. But as the virus spread and changed, the fear became something worse. It was not knowing if, or when, you might get sick. It was not knowing which of your friends might be next. It was being afraid that the world was coming to an end."

"But it didn't," Josh reminded her, looking for anything that might make the conversation less depressing.

"No, it didn't," his mother agreed. "But when I see

people—see you—treating the war like it's fun, it's very upsetting. The war was not fun, Josh. It was not a game. Torching the zombies was something that had to be done, but nobody *liked* doing it."

She paused for a moment, then continued, "I know you think the hologame is exactly the way it was. But you can always turn off a game. We couldn't turn off what was happening to us. We couldn't hit a button and get rid of the stench of burning flesh. We couldn't remove a helmet and be back safe and sound in our rooms. We couldn't hit reset and bring people back from the dead."

She looked right at Josh. "You don't know what it was like, Josh. And no matter how much you play that game, you never will."

Josh nodded. "I guess you're right," he said.

"The game is disrespectful," his mother said. "That's the best way to put it. Turning a war into a game minimizes how horrible it was for the people who fought in it, lived through it—died in it," she finished.

"I never thought of it that way," Josh admitted. "But I'm not killing people. I'm killing meatbags."

"What did you call them?" his mother asked. Her face was reddening.

"It's just what we call the zombies," Josh explained.

"It doesn't mean anything. Besides—"

"Is that what you think your aunt Lucy was?" his mother cut in. "A bag of meat?"

"No!" Josh objected. "But that's different. She was a person."

"*All* the zombies were real people," his mother said. "Every last one of them. Don't you ever forget that."

"I said I was sorry," Josh said defensively. He thought his mother was being a little unreasonable. The z's he torched in the game were not real people.

His mother sighed, and Josh waited for her to tell him he was grounded, or that they were going to take away his computer. He held his breath, hoping his punishment wouldn't be too bad.

"I'm not going to tell you not to play the game anymore," she said. "I've told you how your father and I feel about it. I'm going to leave the decision about whether or not to play up to you."

"Me?" Josh repeated.

His mother nodded. "It's up to you," she affirmed. "And I think you'll make the right decision." She walked to the door. "Dinner's in five minutes."

When she was gone, Josh leaned back in his chair. *The right decision,* he thought. He knew what *she* thought the right decision was. But what did *he* think? After hearing his mother talk about what had happened with Aunt Lucy, he felt horrible about ever having played. He understood now why the game upset his mother so much. But like he'd told her, it was still just a game. Not playing it wouldn't erase what had happened.

He wondered if this was some kind of trick, if his mother was testing him to see what he would do. She'd said the decision was up to him, but if he chose to keep playing, would she punish him anyway?

A beeping sound interrupted his thoughts, and Josh looked over at his desk. The light on his computer screen was blinking, signaling a message. *It's probably Firecracker letting me know what a loser I am,* Josh thought as he went and clicked on the message.

Josh:
Good game. Meet me tomorrow.
1600. Yancy Square Park.
Charlie

Charlie? Josh thought. *Charlie who?*

Then it dawned on him. *The* Charlie. *The best player in the game* Charlie. Charlie wanted to meet *him?* But how did he know who Josh was? Josh read the note over but couldn't make any sense of it. Why had Charlie said "good game" when Josh had blown it? Again.

"This has been a really weird day," Josh told himself as he stood up to go downstairs. "A *seriously* weird day."

4

The boy with the skull mask was the least bizarre of the people waiting on the platform when Josh got off the elevated train at Yancy Street the next afternoon. Two girls dressed identically as baby dolls, complete with pigtails tied with pink ribbons and holding oversized lollipops, turned their heavily made-up faces toward him and laughed loudly as he passed by. A man wearing a Santa suit held a burning stick to his mouth and blew a cloud of fire into the air as a small crowd watched and clapped. When he held out his fur-trimmed hat for them to put coins into it, a little boy not more than five years old snatched it from his hand and ran down the long flight of stairs. Santa followed him, cursing loudly.

Welcome to the Docklands, Josh thought as he descended the opposite set of stairs. It wasn't that the Docklands was dangerous, exactly. It was just weird.

The Docklands was where the city's street people lived—not just the outright homeless (although there were lots of them there) but also the runaways and castoffs and people who didn't fit in anywhere else. Walking around there always made Josh feel like he was at a Halloween party. He wondered why Charlie had chosen this part of town to meet in.

"Hey, guy. Want some dust?"

Josh shook his head at the person speaking to him, a boy about his own age whose skin was the light blue of a Duster. His eyes, like those of everyone who used a lot of dust, were a peculiar mix of iridescent blue and purple swirling around a gold pupil in a hypnotizing pattern. He wore only white leather shorts and a harness from which sprouted a pair of white feathered wings. As soon as Josh passed him, the boy asked the same question of someone else: "Want some dust?"

Josh walked to the corner and entered Yancy Square Park. Like the streets, it was filled with all kinds of people. Some sat or slept on benches. Others stood in small groups, talking loudly and smoking. Josh walked through the park, looking at the faces for someone who might be Charlie. Eventually he came to a large fountain. In the center was a raised cube of brushed aluminum that stood on metal legs a dozen feet tall. Water poured from holes in the cube, falling down into the deep aluminum bowl below. On top of the cube stood the statue of a man.

Josh knew who it was. Drax Jittrund, the most famous Torcher of all time. He had led the forces that had cleaned the city of zombies. He'd fought bravely alongside his men, torching thousands of zombies himself before he'd been bitten during a final mission deep in the city's sewers. He'd ordered his men to torch him.

Josh sat on the edge of the bowl. He looked at his watch. It was just past four. The school day had been torture. All he'd been able to think about was meeting Charlie. As soon as the last bell rang, he'd raced out of there.

"Waiting for someone?"

Josh turned to see a girl looking at him. Her features were Asian, her eyes as dark as her hair. She was dressed in jeans and a white T-shirt underneath a battered leather jacket. The T-shirt said MISSION OF BURMA. Her feet were encased in heavy black boots with thick heels that made her a good five inches taller than she really was.

"A friend," Josh answered. "I'm meeting him here."

"Want to see a trick?" asked the girl. She held out a pack of cards. "Take one."

Josh looked at the cards.

"Go on," the girl said. "Pick one. If I guess right, you give me a dollar. And if I guess wrong, I give you something."

Normally Josh would have walked away. But something about the girl made him want to stay. He liked her, even though he was sure she was scamming him.

"Okay," he said.

He reached out and took a card from the pack the girl had fanned out in her hand. He was surprised to see it wasn't an ordinary playing card but a tarot card with a picture of a stone tower. Lighting was striking the top of the tower, and several people were falling from it. It was a disturbing picture, and Josh found himself wanting to hand the card back.

"Hold on," said the girl. "I haven't guessed yet." She closed her eyes and scrunched up her eyebrows. She made a series of faces, moving her mouth around and seeming to get more and more frustrated. Finally she opened her eyes. "That was hard," she said. "But I think I've got it. You have the eight of pentacles."

Josh shook his head. "Nope," he said. He held the card up so that she could see it.

"The tower," the girl said. She shook her head and sighed. "That one always tricks me." Then her face brightened and she smiled. "But that means *you* win," she told Josh.

Josh smiled. "All right," he said. "So what do I get?"

"How about I tell you where your friend is?" the girl said.

Josh laughed. "You don't even know who I'm waiting for," he said.

The girl looked at him, her eyes sparkling. "Charlie," she said.

Josh stopped smiling. "How did you know that?"

"I know a lot of things, Josh," said the girl.

"How—" Josh started. He stared at her for a moment as his brain put the pieces together. "Wait. *You're* Charlie?"

"Not quite what you expected?" the girl asked.

Josh nodded. "Yeah," he said. "I mean—"

"I know what you mean," said Charlie. "You were expecting someone taller. Now come on. Let's go somewhere we can talk."

Charlie led the way back through the park. When they came to the statue of Drax Jittrund, she stopped and fished some coins from the pocket of her jeans. She tossed them into the water. "For good luck," she told Josh.

Outside the park, Charlie walked about a block

before pushing open the door of a small noodle shop. Josh followed her inside. The air was crazy with the sound of a language he didn't understand. But Charlie spoke to a woman in the same language, and the woman pointed to a table at the back of the crowded room.

"I hope you like dumplings," Charlie said when they were seated. "I ordered some for us."

"Sure," Josh said, shrugging. He couldn't help staring at Charlie.

"What?" Charlie said. "You don't like dumplings?"

"No," Josh said quickly. "It's just that I still can't believe you're a girl."

Charlie rolled her eyes. "Get over it," she said. "That whole 'girls don't game' thing is so 2010."

Josh blushed. "I know," he said. "It's just a surprise, is all."

A waiter set a small cast-iron teapot and two small cups on their table and scurried away. Charlie poured tea into the cups and handed one to Josh. The steam that rose from it smelled like oranges. He held the cup in his hands and breathed it in.

"It's easier if people think I'm a guy," Charlie said. "It might be 2032, but boys still don't like to be beaten by girls. And anyway, I like being invisible."

"Why?" Josh asked.

"It has its uses," said Charlie. "Anyway, I didn't ask you here to talk about me. I want to talk about you. I've been watching you. I like your playing style."

Josh snorted. "Apparently you haven't seen my last few missions," he said.

Charlie nodded. "You had some problems," she said. "It happens. It's not like you have the best partner."

"Firecracker?" Josh said.

"The guy has no style," Charlie said. "He just bull-dozes his way through the missions. If you weren't around, he'd be demoted to noob status in no time."

"I don't think he's *that* bad," Josh said as the waiter returned and set a steaming bowl of dumplings on the table.

"He is," said Charlie, picking up some chopsticks and using them to pluck a dumpling. "But you, you're good."

Josh tried to pick up a dumpling, but it fell. He tried again and failed. But the third time he managed to catch the slippery dumpling between the sticks and raise it to his mouth. He popped it in before it could fall.

"See?" Charlie said. "You're a fast learner."

"Thanks," Josh mumbled as he chewed the dumpling. He didn't know what else to say. Had Charlie really asked him to come down here just to compliment his playing style?

"I have a little proposition for you," Charlie said.

Josh raised an eyebrow. "What kind of proposition?"

"You've heard about the IRL games, right?" she asked in a low voice.

IRL. In real life. *Of course I've heard of them,* Josh thought. Everybody had. Everybody who played the game, anyway. Supposedly there were gamers who got together and played the game for real. The story was that there were still some places in the country where zombies turned up from time to time. When they did, gamers who were in on the secret would go and hunt them down. Only it was an urban legend, like the rats the size of dogs that supposedly lived in the sewers.

"Sure," Josh said. "I've also heard of the sandman and the tooth fairy." He started to pick up another dumpling, but it fell onto the table.

"What would you say if I told you the games *are* real and that I'm inviting you to play?" Charlie asked.

Josh poked at the dumpling, and it slid away from him. "Right," he said, laughing.

Charlie reached out with her chopsticks and expertly scooped up the dumpling. "I only ask once," she said, and put the dumpling in her mouth. "Yes or no?"

Josh stared at her. "You're serious," he said. "You play in the IRL games?"

"Keep it down," Charlie ordered. "You might think no one in here understands you, but you'd be surprised who's listening." She cast an eye at the waiter who was shuttling bowls of noodles from the kitchen to the tables. Then she looked back at Josh. "The games aren't quite what people say they are, but they're pretty close to it. And like I said, I only ask once, so what's it going to be?"

Josh hesitated. He was already pushing things with his parents by playing the online game. What would they say if they knew he was playing it in real life? *But how can you pass this up?* he asked himself. Before he could talk himself out of it, he spoke. "Yes," he said. "Absolutely."

Charlie smiled, although for a moment Josh thought maybe he saw something in her eyes that said she wasn't completely happy that he'd accepted. But then it was gone. "Great," she said. "I knew you would." She stood up. "I've got to go. Meet me in the park tomorrow. Same time."

"Wait," Josh said. He wanted to ask Charlie just *how* real the game was. Like where did the zombies come from? But that was a dumb question. Of course they didn't hunt real zombies. "What should I bring?"

he asked instead. "I mean, I don't have any gear or anything."

"Don't worry about it," Charlie told him. "I'll take care of you. Just show up." She turned to go, then turned back. "And don't tell anyone," she said. "About me or about the game."

Something about the look she gave him chilled Josh. Her eyes were hard, and she wasn't smiling. He nodded quickly. "No worries," he said. "I won't say anything."

Charlie's friendly grin returned. "Great," she said. "I'll see you tomorrow."

Josh watched her go. As soon as the door closed behind her, the waiter came over and slapped down a bill. "Pay up front," he said, frowning.

5

"**W**hat's with you today?"

Josh looked up from his lunch. "Sorry," he said to Firecracker, who was looking at him as he chewed a bite of his sandwich. "What did you say?"

"I said we need to get busy on our planetary geography project," Firecracker said. "Our presentation is tomorrow."

Josh groaned. He'd forgotten about the project. He and Firecracker were supposed to do a report on how Antarctica was becoming a rain forest because of global warming, then do a presentation to the class. But they'd done almost no work on it. Every time they started to, they ended up playing the game instead.

"Tell you what," Firecracker said. "If you do the written paper, I'll do all the presentation stuff. Maps. An animated timeline. Maybe a holographic model. How's that sound?"

"Sure," Josh said. "You're better at the talking part anyway."

"And you're the word guy," Firecracker agreed. "Between us, we're looking at an A."

"A-plus," said Josh.

"So what's going on?" Firecracker asked a moment later. "You've been weird all day."

"No, I haven't!" Josh objected. "I'm just . . . thinking."

"Don't think too hard," said Firecracker. "You'll wear your brain out."

Josh laughed. "You should talk," he fired back.

"It's your mom, right?" said Firecracker. "You feel guilty about her catching you the other night when we were playing the game." He popped a potato chip into his mouth and chewed loudly.

Josh hesitated a moment before answering. Firecracker often had a weird way of knowing what Josh was thinking, but this time he was wrong. Although it was a good guess, what was really bothering Josh was that he couldn't tell Firecracker about his meeting with Charlie. If Firecracker knew the live games were real, he would be even more excited than Josh. But Josh couldn't do anything that would risk Charlie telling him to forget it.

"I guess I feel a little guilty," he lied. "She was really upset."

"Maybe we should lay off for a while," said Firecracker.

"What?" Josh said, shocked to hear Firecracker suggest such a thing.

"Just for a while," said Firecracker. "A week. Maybe two. Long enough for her to forget about it. It's not like we'll die if we don't play." He upended the bag of chips and tapped the remaining crumbs into his mouth.

Josh was about to protest when he realized that Firecracker had just given him the perfect way to hide what he was doing—not from his mother, but from his best friend. Still, he felt like the worst friend in the world as he said, "You're sure you're okay with that?"

Firecracker nodded. "It's no big deal," he said. "Besides, you'd do it for me."

Josh's heart sank. "Thanks," he said as he got up. "I'll talk to you later, okay?"

"You got it," Firecracker said. "You want to check out the new mechaspiders at the Menagerie after school? I'm thinking of getting a tarantula."

"Sorry," Josh said. "That would be cool, but I've got a dentist's appointment."

"Gotcha. I'll call you later tonight, then."

The rest of the day seemed to crawl by, but finally the last class was over and Josh hurried out of school. He avoided his usual route to the subway, taking the long way so he wouldn't run into Firecracker. Only when he was on the train heading downtown did he relax a little bit.

Charlie was waiting for him at the statue of Drax Jittrund. She was wearing pink pants and a bright orange leather jacket over an aqua-blue turtleneck. Her hair was done up in pigtails.

"I thought we were trying to be inconspicuous," Josh said.

"In case you haven't noticed, this *is* inconspicuous in the Docklands," said Charlie. "You ready to go?"

"I don't know," Josh replied sarcastically. "I think I'd rather be doing homework."

Charlie laughed. "Well, I'd hate to lose you to the thrill of working out math equations. Come on."

They left the park and headed into the heart of the Docklands. As they walked through the narrow streets, the shops became more and more unusual. Windows filled with shoes and clothes turned into windows filled with real books and antique toys. Josh stopped to look at an old video-game system. "My grandfather had one of those," he told Charlie. "Can you believe the games used to come on *cartridges*?"

"You can find pretty much anything in the Docklands," Charlie told him, taking him by the arm and pulling him away from the window. "But that's not why we're here."

After about ten minutes of walking, they came to the docks that gave the area its name. This was where the huge ships came to unload their cargo. Josh was a little bit nervous about being in what he'd always been told was a dangerous part of the city.

"Don't worry," Charlie told him. "No one's going to bother us."

Josh started to ask her how she could be so sure about that, but something stopped him. Charlie had a confidence about her that seemed to grow the deeper they moved into the Docklands. It was like she'd lived there her whole life, and it occurred to Josh that maybe she had. After all, he didn't know anything about her.

"Down here," Charlie said, pulling Josh into a narrow alleyway that ran between two buildings. Josh, growing more and more nervous, followed her.

When they reached the end of the alley, Josh realized that one wall had a door set into it. Charlie pulled a key on a chain from inside her turtleneck. She inserted the key into the door's rusted lock and turned it. Josh heard something grind inside the door, and then it swung inward.

"After you," Charlie said with a sweep of her hand.

Josh stepped inside and found himself on a small metal platform. Stairs ran down from it to another landing, and then more stairs continued down from that. Light came in from a dirty skylight revealing a series of platforms and stairs going down seemingly forever. Josh felt a shiver of anxiety pass through him, and he gripped the railing that ran along the exposed side of the platform.

"You're not afraid of heights, are you?" Charlie asked as she stepped inside, closed the door, and locked it.

"Maybe a little," Josh admitted.

"Just don't look down," said Charlie as she started to descend.

Josh followed her as Charlie went down and down and down. "What is this place?" he asked Charlie.

"A playing field," Charlie answered. "You'll see."

Finally they reached the end of the stairs. They were in a concrete passageway. The walls were damp, and here and there water trickled down from the low ceiling. The air was cold and smelled slightly sour. Josh looked up and noticed that there were video cameras every thirty feet or so.

"Looks like someone is keeping an eye on us," he remarked.

Charlie followed his gaze. "Those are left over from

when this place was used by the shipping company," she said quickly. "They haven't worked in years."

The cameras didn't look that old to Josh, but he didn't say anything. He didn't want to get into a disagreement with Charlie over something so stupid.

They came to another set of steps and went up this time. Suddenly the narrow hallway opened into a cavernous space filled with rusted pieces of metal. Lights somewhere far above them illuminated the skeleton of a huge ship occupying the center of the room, and several other smaller ships in various stages of completion were strewn throughout the enormous space. Scaffolding covered them, although it was obvious that no one had worked on the ships in years. Tools of all kinds littered the floor, and thick chains hung from the rafters like gigantic vines.

"Cool, huh?" Charlie said.

"This is amazing," Josh said, turning around and around as he tried to take in everything there was to see. "But we've got to be, what, a couple hundred feet underground? How did this all get down here?"

"They used to build ships here," Charlie explained. "Way back when, before they invented hydrogen-cell technology."

"Yeah," said Josh, eyeing the wooden planks. "These are definitely old school."

"These weren't just regular ships," Charlie explained. "They were used for smuggling. People would secretly build and fill the ships here. Then, when they were done, they flooded the room and the ships were raised up to the surface. There are big doors up there"—she pointed up into the dark—"that open into channels that run to the ocean."

"How do you know all this?" Josh asked.

"Clatter told me," Charlie said.

"I did indeed," said a voice. A moment later a figure emerged from the wreckage of the huge ship and walked toward them. Tall and thin, he was dressed in a strange outfit consisting of a very old-fashioned black suit and a top hat. As he moved he made a strange noise, which Josh soon realized was the rattling of hundreds of keys that were sewn onto his coat. They were the old kind—skeleton keys, Josh thought they were called—with long, thin, round bodies and elaborately curled ends. *That explains his name*, Josh thought.

Clatter had long, dark hair that fell onto his shoulders in limp strands. His skin was pale, and he wore steel-rimmed glasses with gray glass lenses. His hands were encased in black leather gloves, and on one finger he wore a gold ring with a very large red stone. Josh was surprised that Clatter seemed to be only a few years older than he and Charlie were.

"You must be Josh," Clatter said. His voice was silky smooth, almost serpentine, as if the words flowed from his mouth like water. "I've heard so much about you."

"Really?" Josh said, genuinely surprised.

"Charlie says you have great natural talent," Clatter continued. "And she ought to know. She's one of the best I've ever discovered."

Josh looked over at Charlie, who was beaming with pride.

"You must be wondering what you're doing here," Clatter said.

"I hear we're going to play a game," Josh said.

"Perhaps we are," said Clatter, smiling. "As Charlie told you, she is part of a group of people who play the game in its purest form. That is to say, in real life."

Josh nodded. "Right," he said. "She did."

Clatter smiled, his mouth forming a thin line across his face. "Well, you might say that I am the . . . master of ceremonies . . . for these games. I seek out the most talented players and bring them here." He swept his hand around the graveyard of ships. "To the arena."

But what do you get out of it? Josh wondered.

"I enjoy watching players who are good at what they do," said Clatter, seemingly reading Josh's thoughts. "It's a beautiful thing, almost like a . . .

ballet," he concluded. "It gives me pleasure."

Josh looked at Charlie. She gave him a quick nod, as if to say everything was okay.

"So how does this work?" he asked.

"You're eager," Clatter said. "I like that. You're going to play in a game with the rest of the team. After I've observed you in action, I'll decide whether or not you're a good fit. If you are, you'll be asked to join."

"And if you don't think I am?" Josh asked.

Clatter smiled again. "Let's hope that won't be the case," he said.

Josh nodded. "Okay," he said. "When do we play?"

Clatter snapped his fingers, and half a dozen figures materialized from out of the ships. "As I always say, there's no time like the present."

6

The group of figures approached, their faces becoming clearer as they stepped into the light. There were four boys and two girls, all of them around Josh's age. They were dressed in black Torcher uniforms, and they each carried a flamethrower. They flanked Clatter, three on a side, and looked at Josh with unreadable expressions on their faces. Suddenly he was nervous.

"This is my team," Clatter said. He pointed to the first Torcher, a tall, muscular boy with dark brown skin and a thick, pinkish scar running diagonally across the bridge of his nose and down past his lip. "This is Scrawl, the team captain. He's been with me the longest."

Josh nodded at Scrawl, who fixed his dark eyes on Josh and didn't blink. Clatter continued with the introductions. "Then we have Seamus and Finnegan," he said, indicating a short boy with pale skin and black hair and a tall boy with equally pale skin but red hair. "Believe it or not, they're twins."

"Hey," the two boys said in unison, nodding.

"Our last man is Stash," said Clatter. A heavy boy with thick arms, thick legs, and a thick neck looked back at Josh. His fat cheeks were tinged bright pink, and his blond hair was shaved into a crew cut. As Josh watched, he took a handful of nuts out of his pocket, cracked the shell from one, and popped the nut into his mouth. He dropped the shell on the ground.

Pistachio, Josh thought, looking at it. *Stash. Very funny.*

He wanted to laugh, but he knew that would be a mistake. Whatever was happening, everyone was taking it very seriously. He flashed a smile at Stash, who nodded curtly.

"And then we have the ladies," said Clatter. "Allow me to introduce Freya and Black-Eyed Susan."

It was easy to tell which girl was which. One was slight, with long blond hair and bright blue eyes; the other was a beautiful Latina with dark hair and eyes. "Call me Bess," she said. "It takes less time."

"And of course you know Charlie," Clatter concluded. "Now let's get you geared up and get this game going." He clapped his hands together, which seemed to break the spell holding everyone in position.

Scrawl came over to Josh. "Come on," he said. "I'll show you the locker room." He turned back to the others. "The rest of you, go through the hit-and-run drill we practiced last week. I don't want any screwups this game."

Charlie smiled and waved at Josh. "See you soon," she said.

Scrawl walked through the ship graveyard with Josh beside him. Josh wanted to ask all kinds of questions, but he also wanted to look cool and collected, so he said nothing. To his relief, Scrawl did enough talking for both of them.

"So you're Charlie's friend," he said. "I hear you've got a good game going. Well, we've got the best gamers around on this team. You want to play with us, you've got to be *ready*. This isn't some weak-ass holographic game. This is the real thing."

They walked down a short corridor that ended at a wall. There were doors on both sides of the hall. "That's the girls' locker room," Scrawl said, indicating the left-hand door. "And this is ours."

He opened the door into a large room tiled all in white. Rows of lockers lined one wall, and there were long wooden benches bolted to the floor in front of them. On the other side of the room were four bathroom stalls, and through an archway Josh saw what appeared to be a communal shower area.

"I'll skip the guided tour," said Scrawl. "Your locker's over here."

He strode to one of the lockers and opened it. Inside a black uniform was hanging, a pair of black boots on the floor beneath it. "Put those on," Scrawl said, nodding at the contents of the locker.

Josh peeled off his T-shirt and hung it in the locker. Scrawl glanced at it. "You into comics?" he asked, nodding at the Batman logo on the shirt.

"Yeah," Josh said. "Are you?"

"Big-time," Scrawl answered. "Mostly the classic stuff. You ever been to the Pageteria?"

"The paper museum?" said Josh. "No.

Scrawl nodded. "My house is about a block away," he said. "It's great. They have actual newspapers, magazines, anything printed on paper from before Cybooks made them obsolete. They have a great exhibit of comic-book art up right now. You should check it out."

"That sounds cool," Josh said as he removed his shoes, shucked off his pants, and stepped into the one-piece uniform.

"This uniform may not look fancy," Scrawl said as Josh zipped himself up. "But built into the fabric are touch-sensitive threads. They send readings to a monitor back at base. Not only can the monitor read your heartbeat and body temperature, it can tell the difference between me just touching you and you falling down and you getting bit by a z."

Josh rubbed his hands over the uniform's material. The technology Scrawl was describing wasn't new, but he'd never heard of it being used in gaming before. "This is the stuff they make army uniforms out of," he said, impressed.

Scrawl grinned. "Clatter has some major contacts," he said. "Now get your boots on. We've got a game to play."

As they walked back to rejoin the others, Josh asked Scrawl the question he'd wanted to ask since Charlie had told him the game was real. "So if we're Torchers, who plays the zombies?"

"Don't worry about it," Scrawl answered. "Just worry about killing them."

"Well, look at you," Clatter said when Josh and Scrawl arrived. "You already look like one of the gang. All you need is this."

Clatter handed Josh a flamethrower. "You know how to use it, right?"

Josh examined the weapon. "No problem," he said.

"Try it out," said Clatter. "Pretend Seamus is a z. Take him out."

Josh hesitated.

"Just do it," Seamus told him.

Josh aimed the flamethrower at Seamus and pulled the trigger. Nothing happened, but a second later a buzzer sounded and a robotic woman's voice announced, "Torcher Seamus has been killed. I repeat, Torcher Seamus has been killed."

"But how—" Josh said.

"The thrower emits an electronic beam," Freya interrupted him. "If it hits you, it activates the sensors in your suit. As far as the monitor is concerned, you just fried Seamus."

Clatter laughed. "Not to worry," he told Josh, clapping a hand on his shoulder. "I'll go to the monitoring room and reset it. In the meantime, you all get ready to play." He turned to Scrawl. "Play will take place in sections one through four. There are three z's. Understood?"

"Yes."

"Ten minutes, then." Clatter looked at Josh. "Good luck," he said. "I do hope you'll survive."

"I'll try," Josh assured him.

"All right. Huddle up." Scrawl barked his orders like he meant them, and Josh and the others circled around him.

"You guys know what to do," he said, looking at each team member. When he came to Josh he stopped. "You're the new guy," he said. "But that doesn't mean you get to take it easy. This is *your* test, so I expect you to hold your own. Got it?"

Josh nodded. "Got it," he said.

Scrawl held his gaze for a long moment, then said, "Good. Here's the plan. Seamus and Finnegan, you two take section one. Bess and Stash, section two."

Stash groaned. "Not the sewer," he said. "How come I always get the sewer?"

Black-Eyed Susan punched him in the arm. "Maybe because you play like—"

"Section three is Freya's and Charlie's," Scrawl interrupted her.

Freya and Charlie high-fived. "Piece of cake," Charlie said.

Josh had been hoping that Charlie would be with him. It would have been nice to have a familiar face around during his first IRL game. Also, he knew how good she was.

"Josh and I will take section four," said Scrawl.

"What's section four?" Josh asked.

Stash laughed. "You're standing in it," he said.

"The ship graveyard?" Josh said, looking around. "But this place is huge. It will take us hours to cover it."

"Don't worry," said Bess, grinning. "The z's will find you soon enough."

A crackling sound came from out of the darkness, and Josh heard Clatter's voice. "The quarry are being released," he said. "The game will begin in three minutes. I suggest you get moving." Then the lights in the room dimmed, throwing the ships into shadow.

"You heard the man," Scrawl said. "Get your butts in gear."

As the others ran off, Charlie turned and gave Josh a thumbs-up. "Good luck," she called out. "I know you can do it."

Josh nodded. The game was beginning, and just as it did during the hologames, his heart was speeding up as adrenaline coursed through him. He wiped his sweaty hands on his suit and took a deep breath.

"It's go time," Scrawl said. "You know how to do a one-two sweep?"

"One guy goes in and drops, the other is right behind him ready to flame," Josh answered. "You use it when checking a hallway, room, or stairwell."

"Right," said Scrawl. "That's what we're going to do when we can. But a lot of this will be one-on-one. Just us and the meatbags. When that happens, there's just one rule."

"Shoot before they bite," Josh said automatically.

Hearing Scrawl call the z's meatbags made him think of his aunt Lucy and the talk he'd had with his mother, but he pushed that thought from his mind. *It's just a game,* he reminded himself.

"Good man." Scrawl started walking. "Let's head out."

They walked into the gloom, heading for the darker parts of the cavernous space first. Around them, pieces of machinery and the rusting hulls of ships rose up in twisted shapes. Josh kept his eyes and ears open. Although the hologame recreated the experience of being in a real place, this *was* real. He smelled the rusting metal and oil all around him. He felt the dirt and broken pieces of glass and metal under his boots.

He and Scrawl approached the largest ship. "This is as good a place as any to start," he said. "I'll take point."

Josh followed as Scrawl entered the ship through a large hole torn in the hull. As they passed through the ship's belly, Josh kept alert for any sign of zombie action. It was eerily silent, and even Josh's and Scrawl's footsteps were barely more than whispers.

Suddenly a sound came from their right, a noise like metal scraping against metal. Josh whirled and pointed his flamethrower. But Scrawl held out his hand, stopping him. Without saying anything, he nod-ded his head, telling Josh they should keep moving toward the sound.

They crossed the hold quickly but carefully. Josh scanned the floor, making sure he didn't trip over any-thing or give away their approach. Beside him, Scrawl moved catlike through the dark, his flamethrower moving from side to side as he looked for signs of z's.

When they reached a doorway, they stopped. Josh listened. He heard the scraping sound again, but this time it seemed to be above their heads. At first he didn't understand, but then Scrawl pointed up and moved his fingers in a walking motion. *Stairs,* Josh thought. *It's climbing some stairs.*

Scrawl motioned again, indicating that he would go first. He ducked into the stairwell, and Josh fol-lowed. As Scrawl dropped to one knee, Josh readied his flamethrower. But there was no sign of the zombie. Josh looked up and saw that the stairs went up into darkness. He heard something hit the floor above him and roll. Then there was a series of clanks as some-thing fell between the stair railings and hit the next level.

Josh stepped back just as the item tumbled from the darkness and landed where he had been standing. He bent down and looked at it. It was a length of pipe, covered in rust. But something didn't look right about it. Josh reached out and touched the surface. His fingers came away sticky.

Blood, he realized. *One end is covered in blood.* And not just blood. A clump of hair came away from the pipe as well. Josh dropped it in disgust and looked at Scrawl. "That's real blood," he whispered. "Someone is really hurt. We have to help."

He started to go up the stairs, but Scrawl pulled him back. "No," he said quietly. "We have to play the game."

"But whoever that is—"

"It's part of the game," Scrawl said. "Understand?"

Josh began to object, but the tone of Scrawl's voice stopped him. *He's not joking around,* Josh thought.

Scrawl pointed up once more. Then he led as they climbed the stairs. Josh kept his eyes trained up, trying to see through the steps. But there was nothing. And no sound came either.

They climbed one level, then another. There was no sign of the zombie, and Josh's neck hurt from craning his head upward. He was starting to think that the game wasn't going well for him, and that Clatter would tell him he wasn't good enough to be on the team.

When they reached the third level, Josh looked

down to stretch his neck muscles and noticed that the platform was splattered with blood. Following the trail, he saw that it disappeared though a doorway. Tapping Scrawl on the arm, he nodded toward the opening. Then he held up one finger, letting Scrawl know that he would go first.

He stepped through the doorway and went into a crouch. Scrawl stepped in behind him. They were in a hallway. The blood trail continued before them. Josh stood up, and he and Scrawl began to move forward in the dimly lit corridor.

It's got to be here somewhere, Josh thought, trying not to think about how realistic the blood and hair on the pipe had looked.

The hallway ended about twenty yards from where they had entered. In front of them was a door covering a pass-through hatch. It was held closed by five thick bars of steel that radiated out like the arms of a starfish from a central wheel. Turning the wheel would retract the bars and open the door. There was blood on the wheel.

Josh turned to Scrawl. "It's through there," he said. "It must have gone through and closed the door from the other side." It was a pretty smart move for a zombie, and Josh wondered if the person playing the part wasn't being a little too clever.

Scrawl nodded in agreement. "Let's go," he said. "But be careful."

Josh set his flamethrower down. He reached out and, avoiding the blood, tried to turn the big wheel. But it was rusted shut. He put all his weight into it. Soon sweat was running down his face and his muscles ached, but no matter how hard he pushed or pulled, he couldn't budge it.

Suddenly a horrible roar came from behind him. Josh whirled around and saw a zombie standing in the doorway he and Scrawl had just come through. It was a woman. Her long hair was matted, and her face was covered with sores. Above her right eye was a huge gash. Her scalp was torn open. Blood oozed from the wound and ran down her cheek, which was streaked with dried gore. *She really looks like a meatbag,* Josh thought, impressed by all the trouble Clatter had taken to make the game more realistic. Still, Josh was kind of creeped out seeing something so gross in real life.

Scrawl dropped down and aimed his flamethrower at the zombie, who was shuffling toward them. Her mouth was open, and long strings of drool hung from her battered lips. She moaned loudly as she moved. *It almost sounds like she's trying to talk,* Josh thought as he raised his flamethrower.

He waited for Scrawl to shoot. As the Torcher closest to the z, he had first shot. But Scrawl seemed to be struggling with his flamethrower.

"It's jammed!" he cried out. "I can't fire!"

The zombie was getting closer, and the gurgling in her throat was getting louder as she neared her prey. She reached out her hands.

"Torch her!" Scrawl shouted. "Now!"

7

Scrawl flattened himself on the floor of the hallway and covered his head with his arms. Josh aimed his flamethrower at the zombie, who was only a dozen feet away now, and pulled the trigger.

Flames erupted from the end of the torch. Josh watched, shocked, as the ball of flame hurtled toward the z, hit her in the chest, and bloomed. The zombie let out an unearthly scream and began beating uselessly at the flames as they consumed her dress. She staggered back toward the door, her hair blazing and her face engulfed in flames.

Josh could only stare at her burning figure. His eyes saw that the zombie was on fire, but his mind couldn't understand what was happening. *It's not real,* he told himself. *It's just a game. The torch isn't supposed to really work.* Was it some kind of holographic trick? No, it was too real. Had he accidentally been given a real flamethrower instead of an electronic one?

The zombie managed to get out of the hallway, which was now brutally hot and filled with black smoke and the foul stench of burning meat. A moment later Josh heard a muffled *thud*.

"Come on," Scrawl said. "We've got to get out of here."

He and Josh ran for the doorway. When they exited onto the platform, Josh looked over the railing. Far below them the burning body of the z lay on the floor. Then, to his horror, the zombie moved. She pulled herself along with her hands, managing to get about ten feet before collapsing.

Scrawl scrambled quickly down the stairs. Josh followed. When they reached the bottom, they ran to the burning body. It was now nothing more than a charred mess, unrecognizable as anything approaching human. The flamethrower had done its job.

Josh heard a crackling sound. Then the robotic voice he'd heard earlier said, "The quarry has been eradicated. Please report back to the rendezvous site."

The lights went up and Josh blinked as his eyes adjusted. Scrawl turned and started to walk away, but Josh grabbed his arm. "Hold up," he said. "What just happened? That thing was real. The flamethrower is real. It's not supposed to work."

"It's a game," said Scrawl. "That's all."

He pulled his arm away from Josh's grip and kept walking. Josh took one more look at the smoking body of the zombie and trotted after Scrawl.

"*That* is real," he said. "You can't tell me it isn't."

"You did a good job," Scrawl said. "Well, except for taking us into a dead end. But you didn't know the door wouldn't open."

"And you did?" asked Josh.

Scrawl grinned. "Got you," he said. "The whole thing was set up to see how you'd do."

Josh's mouth fell open. "Then the z wasn't—"

"Cybernetic," Scrawl told him. "Clatter's a robotics genius. He builds them for fun. Pretty real, huh?"

Josh sighed. "Too real," he said. "I just about lost it when the torch shot flame."

Scrawl laughed. "I did too the first time," he said. "That's another of Clatter's tricks. He switches it on from the monitoring room."

"But I could have torched you!" Josh objected.

"No chance," said Scrawl. "Well, maybe a *small* chance, but Clatter doesn't make it live until he's sure you're in position and anyone with you is out of the way."

Josh found himself laughing with relief.

"The guy's a little bit nuts," said Scrawl. "But you've got to admit, that was intense."

"Yeah," Josh agreed. "It was."

"You liked it," said Scrawl. "I can see it in your eyes."

Josh hesitated a moment. "Yeah," he said again. "I did."

They walked in silence until they got back to the starting point. Clatter and the other team members were there. When Josh drew near they all started clapping loudly. Charlie came up and high-fived him. "I knew you'd do it," she said. Then she grinned. "Of course when *I* did my first run, I nailed the meatbag in about half that time."

"That was very good work," Clatter told Josh.

"That was a very realistic zombie," Josh replied.

Clatter laughed. "It's nothing," he said, although he sounded pleased. "Just a little hobby."

Josh looked at the others. "So you were all in on this?"

Black-Eyed Susan laughed. "Consider it your initiation," she said.

"We were all watching from the monitor room," Finnegan explained. "You really kept your cool."

"Yeah," said Freya. "When Stash did his first run,

he saw the z and just about burned my hair off."

Stash spat a shell toward Freya. "My meatbag was way scarier than his," he said sullenly.

The others laughed, and Josh saw Stash shoot him a look. *I don't think he and I are going to be best buds,* he thought.

"So, Josh, do you want to join our merry band?" Clatter asked.

Josh nodded. "But I still don't really get what you all do. This seems like a lot of work just to play the game."

"Ah," said Clatter. "That's very perceptive of you. You're quite right. But you see, this is more than just a game."

"I don't understand," Josh said.

Clatter came closer. "Before I explain further, I require your promise that whatever is said here remains here."

"Sure," Josh said.

Clatter cocked his head. "I'm very serious," he said. "Don't answer lightly. Should you break your promise, the ramifications are very . . . unfortunate."

"He means if you shoot your mouth off about this, we'll make sure your reputation in the game community is dirt," Seamus said.

Josh hesitated. They were taking everything really

seriously for it being a game. He wondered if he'd gotten himself in over his head. But it didn't seem like he could back out now. "It's okay," he said. "I don't talk."

"Excellent," said Clatter. "Because Seamus is right. I've invested a great deal in this operation, and there are people who would dearly love to know how I've achieved what I have. It's a business, and a very lucrative one."

"A business," Josh repeated. "You mean people pay to play it? To play against us?"

"Actually, they pay to *watch* you play it," said Clatter. "And they make bets as to who will make the most kills in a game."

"Gambling," Josh said.

"I prefer to call it wagering," said Clatter. "It's more . . . civilized. We hold games, and people come to watch them. They place bets on the team as a whole or on individual players."

"Or on the meatbags," Stash added.

"Or on the zombies," Clatter agreed.

Josh thought about this for a moment. "But if you make the zombies and you own the team, how do the gamblers know you haven't rigged everything?"

"The *wagerers*," said Clatter, "have generally had other dealings with me. They know me to be a man in whom they can place the utmost trust."

"And it's all legal?" Josh asked. "I won't get into any trouble?"

Clatter smiled. "I admit that not every aspect of my operation is, shall we say, completely approved by the authorities. As you know, the topic of zombies is a very touchy one. I'm afraid there are some people who—if they knew about this—would call for us to be shut down due to their own ignorance and fear. But I assure you that I take very good care of my team. You have no need to worry." He paused for a moment. "And of course you will share in the rewards of our success."

"You mean I'll get paid?" said Josh, surprised.

Clatter nodded. "As a junior member of the team, you'll receive base pay of two percent of the take. In addition, you will receive a bonus for each zombie you dispatch during a game. And occasionally a wagerer will take a liking to a particular player and tip handsomely."

"Wow," Josh said. "Getting paid to play the game. That's pretty cool."

"We generally play one or two times a week," Clatter continued. "I arrange the games so they interfere with your outside life as little as possible."

Josh shrugged. "I guess I don't have any reason to

say no," he said. "I'm in."

A smile spread across Clatter's face. "I'm very pleased to hear it," he said. "Welcome to the team."

The others came and one by one shook his hand. When it was Stash's turn he gripped Josh's fingers tightly and gave them a painful squeeze, smiled stiffly, and said, "Good to have you." Everyone else seemed genuinely glad to have him aboard.

After Josh had been given an electronic-reader card containing a handbook to study, he and Charlie left the building together. This time they exited through a door that led to the back of a warehouse filled with boxes marked TEA.

"There are a dozen or so ways in and out," Charlie explained as they made their way to the street. "Some of them are in the handbook, but some you'll only find out about when somebody shows you. By the way, make sure you memorize the handbook. You'll have to give it back next time we meet."

"Tell me how you started playing," Josh said.

"Bess recruited me," Charlie answered. "We played together in a hologame group."

"How long have you been doing it?"

"About a year," she said.

"And the others?" asked Josh. "Have they all been playing that long?"

Charlie shook her head. "They come and go," she told him. "People burn out or move away. The only ones still here from when I joined are Scrawl and Bess."

"Scrawl seems like an interesting guy," said Josh.

"He used to be a tagger," said Charlie. "A graffiti artist. That's how he got his nickname. Clatter caught him tagging one of his buildings and trained him to be a Torcher. He's nice like that. I know Clatter looks kind of weird, but he's been great to me."

"I don't think Stash likes me much," Josh admitted.

Charlie laughed. "Stash doesn't like anybody. Or at least he pretends not to. I think really he just doesn't know how to have friends. His family is kind of messed up. His dad is in prison for murder, and his mom is a drunk. He's the youngest of six kids. The others all left, and he's the one looking out for his mother. So don't take it personally. He's just not good at trusting people."

"It sounds like there are a lot of stories on the team," Josh said.

"There are," said Charlie. "Finnegan and Seamus had a little trouble with setting things on fire and ended up in juvie. Clatter managed to get them out. They live with him, and he's teaching them all about robotics. Freya's dad is an ambassador. She got kicked out of three or four boarding schools, so now she lives with her dad, but he's never around, and he has no idea whether she's home or not."

"And Black-Eyed Susan?"

"Bess?" Charlie said. "She's kind of a mystery. No one really knows where she lives. Personally, I think she's a runaway."

"So what's your story?"

Charlie grinned. "Mine's pretty boring. Family I like. Good grades. No sociopathic tendencies. I'm just really good at playing the game."

"Same here," Josh said. "I guess we're the token normals."

They stopped in front of a subway entrance. "This is me," she said. "Go home and read the manual. Com me if you have any questions. Clatter will let us know when the next game is."

"Will do," said Josh. "Oh, and thanks for inviting me to play. This is going to be fun."

Charlie smiled. "It will be better than anything you could ever imagine," she said.

8

Josh slipped the card into his reader and waited for it to load. Ever since he got home, he'd been dying to look at the manual, but first he'd had to sit through dinner with his family, and then he'd had to do his math homework. But now all that was done, and he could devote his attention to more interesting matters.

The first section was standard Torcher information, basically an outline of the Rules. Josh already knew these by heart, so he skipped ahead to the next section, which was a description of the various zones in the playing field. In addition to the underground area in the Docklands, Clatter had set up three or four smaller fields throughout the city. One of them used the maze of underground tunnels beneath the abandoned Central Station, another was laid out in the ruins of the Great Park at the northern tip of the city.

Josh pored over the different maps with growing excitement. He couldn't believe Clatter's operation was so extensive. *This is going to be so cool,* he thought as he tried to memorize as many details of the maps as he could. He wanted to impress the others the next time they played.

As he was looking at a map of the sewers that ran beneath the ship graveyard, the telecom sounded an incoming call. "Firecracker is calling," the machine's voice said. "Firecracker is calling."

Josh went to his desk and hit the answer key. Firecracker's face filled the screen. "How's the paper going?" he asked.

Josh wracked his brain. "The paper," he said, a sinking feeling growing in the pit of his stomach.

"Right," Firecracker said. "Did you get your part done?"

"Just about," Josh lied. "I'm still researching a couple of things, but I'm almost finished."

"All right," said Firecracker. "Make sure it's good. My presentation is going to kick major butt, but it's only half the grade. Don't forget you have to submit the written report to Darjeeling by eight tomorrow. She's going to have them graded before we do the presentations."

"Don't worry," Josh said. "It'll be done."

"Okay," Firecracker said. "I'll see you tomorrow. Firecracker out."

The screen went dark, and Josh groaned. He'd forgotten all about the paper. He looked at the clock. It was almost ten. Reluctantly he closed the manual he'd been reading and started to pull up information on Antarctica.

His computer beeped, signaling an incoming message. He opened it and saw a note from Charlie.

The next game is Saturday. Meet me at the park at 1400 hours. Study the maps for Location 4.

Saturday? That's the day after tomorrow, Josh thought. That didn't give him much time, especially since Friday night was family night, when he and Emily were forced to do something with their parents. *You can't show up unprepared,* he told himself.

He started to pick up the manual again, then remembered the planetary geography paper. *Paper first.*

He worked quickly, locating the information he needed and cobbling it into something that resembled a paper. When he was done he read it through. It wasn't his best work, but at least it was finished. Hopefully it was enough to get them a decent grade.

He glanced at the clock and was shocked to see that it was after one o'clock. He was exhausted, but he forced himself to open the manual file and start reading again. Location Four was also in the Docklands. It was an old amusement park called Happy Time that had been built along the boardwalk. Since the ocean around the city had become too polluted to swim in, nobody went there anymore, and like everything in that part of the city, the boardwalk—and Happy Time— had been left to slowly fall apart. Josh had never been there, although his parents had told him and Emily stories about going there when they were kids.

According to the manual, there were a number of buildings still standing at the park, as well as several underground tunnels that must have been used for maintenance purposes. They formed a complex maze that Josh found difficult to keep straight, so in order to memorize them he focused on one section at a time, taking in the details and then closing his eyes and trying to re-create the map in his mind.

The problem was that every time he closed his eyes, he felt himself drifting into sleep. Several times he woke with a jerk, having dozed off in the middle of trying to picture a stairwell or hallway. Then one time he closed his eyes and didn't wake up.

Josh dreamed about trying to find his way out of a

dank cellar. He'd lost his bearings and no longer knew where the stairs he'd come down were. Things were moving in the dark, and he couldn't remember how to use his flamethrower. Hands were grabbing at him, and he felt cold breath on his face. The alarm clock jolted him awake.

He sat up and looked around his room, his heart racing. The dream had been so real. There was a knock on the door, and Emily looked in.

"Are you okay?" she asked.

"Sure," said Josh. "Why?"

"You were yelling in your sleep," his sister told him.

"Oh," said Josh. "It was just a nightmare."

Emily nodded. Then she noticed the reader lying next to Josh on the bed. She came in and picked it up. "What are you reading?"

"No!" Josh yelled, grabbing the reader from her.

"Ohhh," Emily said, a grin spreading across her face. "You were looking at something *naaauugh*-ty!"

"I was not!" Josh countered. "It's just something for school."

"Okay," Emily said, giving Josh an exaggerated wink. "Sure."

"Get out of here," said Josh. "I have to get dressed."

Emily scurried out, laughing, and shut the door. Josh looked at the reader. It was still open to the map of Location Four. Close call. If Emily had seen the map, she definitely would have asked a lot of questions.

Twenty minutes later Josh was downstairs having breakfast. Emily looked at him from across the table and smiled sweetly. "Read any good books lately?" she asked.

Josh glowered at her.

"Don't forget, tonight is family night," his father said. "We're going to go play mini golf."

"Yay!" Emily said, genuinely excited by the news. Josh was a little excited too. Mini golf was super old-fashioned, but it was also kind of cool. He would never let his parents know, but secretly he was looking forward to it.

Fortunately for him, the mini golf news also made Emily forget all about the reader. On the train to school all she talked about was how much fun it was going to be. When she got off at her stop, she waved good-bye to Josh and ran to catch up with some of her friends who had been riding in the car ahead of theirs.

The rocking motion of the train almost lulled Josh back to sleep, and he was glad when he reached his stop and could get out into the cool air.

Firecracker caught up with him as Josh was opening his locker. "Did you get it done?" he asked.

"I did," Josh answered. "*And* I sent it to Darjeeling. The rest is up to you."

"Piece of cake," said Firecracker. "I'll see you later."

The day dragged on. At lunch Josh tried to perk himself up by downing an energy drink, but all it did was make him feel sick. By the time planetary geography class rolled around in the afternoon, he was both wired and sleepy. It was a horrible combination, and all he wanted to do was sit at his desk and zone out.

Unfortunately, he had to listen to the other presentations. There was going to be a test on the information, so he forced his eyes open and tried to concentrate on what was being said. Beside him, Firecracker's leg bounced up and down anxiously as he waited his turn to go before the class.

Josh listened as Veda Churling told them about the formation of the Martian Sea, then as Peter Prieboy gave a rambling account of the meteor strike that had created the Vargas Canyon. None of it was very interesting, and Josh found his thoughts wandering. He hoped the recorder built into his NoteTaker had caught everything, but he doubted it. It had been acting up lately, and he hadn't had time to fix it.

Finally it was Firecracker's turn. He went to the front of the room and started talking. As promised, he had made holographic maps to illustrate the changes taking place in Antarctica and how the resulting rise in water levels was affecting the rest of the earth. This was followed by an animation showing the Antarctic Conflict waged by the seven countries claiming territorial rights to the area, and the ultimate creation of a protected world park there.

When Firecracker was done, the class applauded. Firecracker took a deep bow, waving to his audience and hamming it up. Josh couldn't help but laugh. They were going to get a great grade, he just knew it.

With the presentations over, Ms. Darjeeling resumed control of the class. "I have to say, I'm very impressed with your work on these projects," she told them. "I'm sending your grades to your NoteTakers. If you have any questions about them, please see me after class."

She punched a sequence of numbers into the control panel on her desk, and all around the room NoteTakers made the chiming sound that indicated the arrival of a transmission. Josh clicked on his message box and looked for his grade.

When he saw it, his heart skipped a beat. He'd expected a B-plus or at worst a B. He'd gotten a D.

"I got an A," Firecracker said. "Score one for me. What did you get?"

"Not an A," Josh said.

Firecracker looked at Josh's screen. "A D?" he said loudly enough for several people to look over at them. "Our final grade is based on *both* our scores. That means we're getting a . . ."

"C-plus," said Josh as Firecracker tried to figure out the answer in his head.

"A C-plus," Firecracker agreed.

"A C-plus isn't *that* bad," said Josh, trying to reassure his friend.

"It's not an A," Firecracker shot back.

"I'm sorry," said Josh. "I don't know what happened. I thought I did an okay job."

"Yeah, well, apparently you didn't," Firecracker said, slumping in his seat. "Thanks a lot, partner."

"I'm sorry," Josh said again. But Firecracker wouldn't even look at him.

9

"**W**hat's the matter, cowboy?"

Josh looked up. Charlie was standing in front of him on the train. "What are you doing here?" he asked her, looking around.

"Relax," Charlie said. "Your friend isn't here."

"Did you follow me?" Josh said.

Charlie smiled. "Why would I do that?" she replied. She took the seat next to Josh. "Okay, maybe I did. But I'm not stalking you or anything. I just wanted to see if you could come over tonight."

"Come over?" Josh repeated.

"To my house," Charlie clarified. "I thought we could go over the maps for tomorrow."

Josh shook his head. "I can't," he said. "Tonight is family night."

Charlie raised an eyebrow. "Family night," she said. "Sounds fun."

"Yeah. Well." Josh shrugged. He didn't want to tell Charlie he was actually looking forward to mini golf. Or at least he *had* been, until he'd gotten the grade on his report. Now he didn't really feel like doing anything.

"This is a big game for you," Charlie reminded him. "And Location Four isn't the easiest field to play. Are you sure you're ready?"

Josh started to assure her that he was, but found himself saying, "Actually, no. I'm not sure at all. I tried to memorize the maps last night, but I had to do this report for school, and it got late and—"

"You're coming over," Charlie interrupted him. "Just tell your parents you have to do something else tonight."

"Like what?" said Josh.

Charlie thought for a moment, biting her lip and frowning. "Tell them you're volunteering for something," she said. "Tonight is orientation, and tomorrow is your first day. That gives you an out for both days. And whenever we have a game, you can say you have to volunteer."

"I don't know," Josh hedged. "I don't think they'd buy it."

"Tell them it's for school credit," said Charlie.

Josh thought about it. "That *might* work," he

agreed. "But I need to think of a realistic group to volunteer for."

"The homeless," said Charlie. "You're helping the homeless. That's perfect. You can tell them the group works all over the city; that way they won't ever expect you to be in any one place."

Josh knew Charlie was right that he was going to need a good excuse for spending time away from home. He took a deep breath, then dialed his mother's number at work and told her what he was supposedly doing.

"That went well," Charlie remarked when Josh ended the call.

"I lucked out," said Josh. "She was distracted. One of the gryphons bit someone."

"Gryphons?" Charlie said.

"She's a biologist," Josh explained. "A cloner. She makes imaginary animals. I mean she makes imaginary animals *real*."

"I get it," said Charlie. "Cool. What does your dad do?"

"He's a doctor too," said Josh. "The normal kind. You know, shots and checkups and stuff."

"Wow," Charlie said. "Two brainiacs for parents. Did you inherit their superbrains?"

Josh laughed. "Not so much," he said. "My sister

Emily is the smart one. She's actually scary smart. I'm pretty good at a lot of things, but not super good at any of them."

"Except torching," Charlie reminded him.

"Except that," Josh agreed. "So what do your parents—"

"This is our stop," said Charlie, interrupting. She stood up as the doors opened, and she and Josh hopped off. Charlie pointed to a train on the other side of the platform. "Come on," she said. "That's the one we want."

The second train took them diagonally across the city, going underground for most of the way and then emerging into daylight and climbing up onto the elevated tracks. Below them Josh saw the squat, brown brick houses of Old Town. The steel supports of the elevated train stuck up like the legs of giant birds from the tangle of homes.

Old Town occupied the northeast corner of the city. Most of the houses were the original ones built hundreds of years before by the settlers who discovered the land. They were all built with bricks made from local clay, which gave them their brown color. Josh had been there a few times, mainly to visit the Museum of City History on school trips. But he didn't know anyone who lived there.

"Here we are," Charlie said as the train came to a stop. They exited onto a platform high above the street and headed for the stairs.

They walked to Charlie's house, passing lots of cafes where people sat drinking, smoking, and talking loudly. Then they turned a corner and came to a house that looked just like all the other houses in the neighborhood, with one notable difference; the front gate was made of wrought iron and topped with a big black bird whose eyes—made of copper—seemed to stare at Josh menacingly.

"My dad made it," Charlie said, as if she was used to explaining the bird. "He's a sculptor. Iron, mostly."

"It's cool," Josh said, but the truth was that he found the bird more than a little creepy.

They went up a short flight of steps to the front door, and as they stepped inside Charlie called out, "Dad?"

There was no answer.

"Come up to my room," Charlie said, heading for a set of stairs.

Josh followed her. The wood of the stairs was old and well worn. Centuries of use had made the wood smooth, and there were deeper indentations in the center of each step where people had most often placed their feet.

"This is my dad's studio," Charlie said as they arrived at the second floor. It was one huge space, with bare brick walls and a floor covered with white canvas cloths. A workbench cluttered with tools lined one wall, and in the center of the room stood a sculpture made of bits and pieces of metal, all welded together to form what looked like a human figure. But something was wrong with it. It was twisted, the arms seeming to reach out to grab something.

"My bedroom is on the third floor," Charlie said, walking past the sculpture without looking at it. They went up another flight of stairs and down a hallway. "That's my dad's room," Charlie said as they passed a closed door. "This is mine." She opened a door on the opposite side of the hall and went inside. The room also had bare brick walls, and at one end, farthest from the windows, a huge bed made out of iron stood against the wall.

"Another of my dad's creations," said Charlie. She went to a console on the wall, pressed some buttons, and music began to play. It was a song Josh had never heard, with lots of loud guitars and wild drumming.

"What is this?"

"It's old," Charlie said. "A band my grandmother used to listen to called the New York Dolls. I'm kind of into it." She danced around as the music played, throwing her head from side to side. "Sorry," she said, falling on the bed. "You must think I'm nuts."

"No," Josh said, laughing. "I think you're cute." Immediately he realized what he'd said. "I mean, um, we should go over the maps," he said quickly.

"Did you just say you think I'm cute?" Charlie asked.

"No," Josh said.

"So you *don't* think I'm cute?" asked Charlie.

"No," Josh replied. "I mean, yeah. But I didn't mean it to come out that way."

"It's okay," she said. "I think you're cute too."

Before Josh could respond, Charlie jumped up. "Stay here," she said. "I'll be right back."

Josh felt his cheeks flush as he tried to process what had just happened. He *did* think Charlie was cute, but he hadn't meant to tell her that. It had just slipped out, and now he couldn't take it back. *Now what?* he thought.

Charlie returned to the room carrying a box. She brought it to the bed and set it down. It was made of black metal, and the surface was scratched and dented. In the center of the top was a logo Josh recognized at once—a simple circle with flames in it.

"That's the Torcher symbol," he said.

Charlie nodded. "My dad was a Torcher," she told

him as she lifted the lid. "He kept some stuff."

She reached into the box and pulled out a small cyphoto album. Starting it up, she showed Josh the screen. On it was a photo of seven men all wearing Torcher uniforms. They grinned happily at the camera.

"That's his squad," Charlie said.

"Which one is your dad?" Josh asked.

Charlie pointed to a short man with black hair. He was the only one not smiling. "There," she said.

She scrolled through the pictures. Mostly they were of the men from the first photograph. Then they came to a picture showing a beautiful woman. She was leaning against a railing. Behind her Josh could see the tracks of a roller coaster, and to one side three little kids ran by in a blur, balloons bobbing on the strings in their hands. The woman was holding a cone of bright pink cotton candy.

"That's my mom," Charlie said.

"That roller coaster looks familiar," said Josh.

"It's Happy Time," Charlie said quietly. "My dad took her there when he asked her to marry him." She stared at the picture for a long time without saying anything.

"What happened to her?" Josh asked finally.

Charlie turned the album off. "She died," she

said. She put the album back in the box and took out something else. It was a medal. "My dad got this for torching a thousand z's," she said, handing it to Josh. "Isn't it cool?"

Josh examined the medal. It was round, and in the center was the Torcher logo. Beneath it was the Torcher motto: SAVED BY FIRE.

"He must have saved a lot of people," Josh said, impressed.

"You mean zombies," Charlie countered.

Josh looked at her, not understanding.

"Think about it," said Charlie. "Zombies used to be people. By killing them, the Torchers saved them from having to be monsters."

"I always thought that by the time z's turned they were pretty much not human anymore," Josh said.

"You don't know that," Charlie said, her voice oddly sharp. "Nobody really knows." She took the medal back and returned it to the box.

"Can I ask you something?" Josh said.

Charlie nodded.

"How come when you play the hologame, you always play a meatbag?"

"It's good training," said Charlie. "It helps me learn to think like a zombie, so when I play the game for real I get inside their heads."

"I don't think I want to be in a head like that," Josh told her.

Charlie looked at him. "Don't knock it till you've tried it," she said. "You might even *like* it."

Charlie got up and walked to her dresser. Opening the top drawer, she rooted around and pulled something out. When she came back, Josh saw that she was holding a small silver vial.

"What is that?" he asked.

Charlie unscrewed the top of the vial and poured two small, white tablets into her palm. "This," Charlie said, "is Z. It's something that will help you think like a zombie. At least for a little while. I take it whenever I'm playing the game."

Josh eyed the pills doubtfully. "I don't do drugs," he said.

"Don't worry," Charlie said. "It's totally safe. It's not a *drug* drug." She took one of the pills and put it in her mouth. She swallowed and stuck out her tongue. "See? Now it's your turn."

She handed Josh the second pill. He held it between his fingers, looking at it. Was it really safe? What was it going to do to him? He looked at Charlie, who laughed. "Come on," she said. "You won't regret it."

That's what they all say, Josh thought. *Right before you do something stupid.* But he had to admit, he was curious. Also, he didn't want Charlie to think he was afraid.

"It will make me think like a zombie?" he asked.

Charlie nodded.

"And that's a *good* thing?"

"Just trust me," said Charlie. "It's like nothing you've ever done."

Josh looked at her face. She was grinning. *How bad can it be?* he thought. Before he could answer that question, he put the pill in his mouth and swallowed.

10

"Josh! Dinner!"

Josh closed his eyes. He wasn't really in the mood to be with his family, but he had no choice. He'd come home early from Charlie's, totally forgetting that he wasn't supposed to be done with his fake meeting until eight. When he walked in, his parents and Emily were there. The mini-golf place had been closed for renovations, so they'd come home to have dinner and play some board games.

They were all happy to see him, but he wished he were anywhere else but there. *I should have stayed at Charlie's,* he thought. But Charlie had homework to do. She'd promised to call later to see how he was doing. "In the meantime," she'd said, "just go with it."

He'd started to feel weird on the train ride home. It wasn't anything he could put his finger on. He just started to feel kind of . . . fuzzy. The feeling had grown stronger, and now he felt slightly nauseated. The last thing he wanted to do was eat.

At the same time, though, he was starving. He hadn't realized how hungry he was, but now he was acutely aware of the rumbling in his stomach. It felt as if he hadn't eaten in days.

He checked his face one more time. Seeing nothing out of the ordinary, he left his room and went downstairs. His father was standing at the stove. The grill in the center of the range was lit, and the smoke from it was being sucked up into the silver hood that covered the stove.

"You're just in time," said Josh's father as he placed one of the steaks on the grill. It sizzled as it touched the hot metal.

Josh looked at the cooking meat, and his mouth began to water as the smell filled his nose. The scent was incredibly strong—blood and fat and meat mingled together. He swallowed hard, tasting it in his throat.

"How would you like your steak prepared this evening, sir?" his father asked him. "Medium or well done?"

"Rare," Josh answered. "Almost raw."

His father looked at him with a surprised expression. "You sure?" he asked.

"I'm sure," said Josh.

"You're the boss," his father said as he laid two other steaks on the grill.

He poked the steaks with a fork. Juice ran from the holes and fell onto the grill, popping and hissing. Each crackle released another burst of the meaty smell, making Josh swallow hard as he imagined putting the meat in his mouth and chewing it. He had to force himself not to snatch the remaining raw steak from the plate and start gnawing on it.

It must be the Z, he realized. *It's working*.

Charlie had told him that the drug made you feel wild. Now Josh understood what she meant. He did feel wild, almost animal-like. He could still think, but another part of him was growing more powerful by the minute, a part he had never experienced so clearly before. He felt his heart racing.

"Here, you take over."

Someone was speaking to him. Josh looked at the speaker, and for a moment he couldn't tell who it was. He saw a faceless body, a body that coursed with blood and smelled the same as the meat on the grill. Then his vision cleared, and he realized that he was looking at his father. He was holding the meat fork out to Josh.

"Oh," Josh said, trying to remember where he was.

"Yeah. I'll do it." He took the fork from his father and went to stand in front of the grill.

"I'm going to go help your mother set the table," his father said. "Let those cook another couple of minutes, then turn them over. Put your steak on when you flip those, and turn it after two minutes."

Josh nodded. His father left him alone, and he stood staring at the cooking meat. Once again the amazing smell overwhelmed him. He reached out with the fork and pierced one of the steaks. Juice dripped onto the grill, where it bubbled and blackened. The rest pooled on top of the meat. Josh touched it with his fingertip and ran it over his lips, smearing them with blood. His tongue flicked out and licked it off. The iron taste filled his mouth, and he wanted more.

His steak was still waiting to go on the grill. Instead of putting it on, he took a knife and cut off a large chunk. Shoving it into his mouth, he chewed it with big bites, his teeth shredding the meat into pieces that he gulped down greedily. It was amazing, and he picked up the knife to cut some more.

"Are you eating *raw* meat?"

Emily was standing in the doorway, looking at Josh with an expression of disgust. "Do you know what lives in meat?" she said. "You could totally get worms."

Josh heard her talking, but he was more interested

in the way she smelled. Like the steak, she reeked with the aroma of blood. He could hear her heart beating. No, he could *feel* her heart beating, pushing blood through her veins.

"Hello?"

Josh shook his head to clear it. Emily was pointing to the grill, where the steaks were starting to smoke. Josh looked at them for a moment, not realizing what was happening. Then something in his mind turned back on, and he understood that he needed to do something. He quickly flipped the steaks over. The sides that had been against the grill were blackened.

"Mom's going to kill you," Emily decreed before turning around and marching out of the room.

Josh turned his attention back to the steaks. He added his own to the grill and tried to ignore the smell. Something weird was definitely going on in his head, and he knew it had to be the Z. *It's your reptile brain taking over,* he told himself. He didn't know whether that was true or not, but whatever it was, it felt really weird. Weird and kind of exciting. It was as if he'd become somebody else—no, *something* else.

That thing was still inside of him, and it was growing stronger. Slowly Josh felt the part of his brain that could think clearly shutting down as the other, wild part took over. Everything grew a little hazy as his eyesight changed but his sense of smell intensified.

"Josh, are those steaks done?"

He heard his mother's voice, but when he answered her all that came out was a growling sound.

"They smell done," said his mother. "I think they're ready."

Josh managed to get the steaks off the grill and onto a plate, but the smell was almost too much for him. He had to push himself away from the counter before he tore into all four steaks. As it was, he grabbed his own steak and ran with it into the bathroom. Slamming the door, he sat down on the floor and began devouring the meat.

He held the steak in both hands, ripping at it with his teeth. It was still mostly raw, and blood dripped from the shredded pieces. He barely tasted the chunks of meat as he swallowed them, almost choking. He'd never been so ravenous in his life.

A banging on the door stopped him. "You all right in there?" his father called out.

Josh looked at the steak in his hands. Blood covered his fingers, and there were chunks of meat on the floor around him. He stopped himself from picking them up and eating them.

"I'm okay," he answered his father. He had to concentrate hard on speaking the words.

"Well, don't stay in there all night," his father said. "Dinner's ready."

Josh said nothing, but he heard his father walk away. He looked once more at the steak in his hands. There was very little of it left—mostly fat and some stringy pieces covered in blood. Looking at it made him both sick and hungry. Before he couldn't resist any longer, he dropped the remaining meat into the toilet. He scooped up the pieces on the floor and added them as well, then flushed the whole mess down. He watched the meat swirl around the bowl and disappear.

He went to the sink and turned on the cold water. Bending down, he put his mouth under the tap and let the water fill it. It washed away some of the meat taste, but not all of it. He drank some more, swallowing and trying to rinse the blood from his throat. He suddenly felt like he might throw up.

He turned the water off and looked at himself in the mirror. His pupils were huge black circles.

The wild feeling was still there, waiting. As sick as he felt, there was something really exciting about letting that other part of him take over for a little while. Everything felt more real, more raw, more alive.

If that's what being a zombie felt like, he was surprised. He'd always thought of them as being stupid, mindless things that didn't know what they were doing and didn't feel anything. But he felt so much. All he *did* was feel. Every sensation was intense beyond words. And he didn't need words because there was no reason to *think* about anything.

Next time it will be easier, he told himself. *I'll be ready.*

He washed his hands, checked his eyes to see if his pupils were any smaller (they were, a little), and got ready to join everyone for dinner. He didn't know what he was going to say about the steak, but he would come up with something. He would be funny, and they would all have a good time.

Charlie was right—there was nothing to worry about. The Z had been a little intense, but nothing too heavy. Best of all, he had *enjoyed* it, and it really had opened his mind up to what it might feel like to be a zombie. He could see why Charlie took it while she was playing the game. It really made you think like a z did.

He thought about the game tomorrow. It was going to be great. He laughed. His life had changed radically over the past few days. "And this is just the beginning," he told his reflection.

II

It was raining hard the next morning. The wind blew the water across the beach in heavy sheets, carrying with it discarded candy wrappers, empty cans, and other trash that littered the sand. The ocean lapped at the shore with dirty brown tongues flecked with yellowish foam. A dead gull, its feathers matted and torn, was dragged into the water by a wave.

Josh wiped his hair from his eyes and looked for the entrance to Happy Time. He spotted it a little way down the boardwalk—a huge grinning clown's head, its paint worn away so that it had only one eye. Josh carefully made his way along the dilapidated boardwalk. Passing through the clown's open mouth, he walked among the arcade of empty booths until he found one marked with a torn poster of a bearded lady. **OME SEE THE FREAK SHO**, it declared in big letters. To the right of the sign was a doorway covered by a dirty, yellowed curtain. Josh pushed through it and into the room beyond.

"You're late." Stash looked at Josh and popped a nut into his mouth.

"Five minutes," Josh shot back. "The train sat in the tunnel for twenty minutes. I guess the tracks were flooded."

"It's no problem," Bess assured him. She was just pulling on the heavy black boots that went with their uniforms. She gave Stash a scowl. "Besides, Scrawl isn't even here yet, so settle down."

Stash turned away and walked over to a battered old sofa upholstered in red velvet. When he sat on it, a cloud of dust rose around him. He started sneezing violently.

"Serves him right," Bess said, laughing. "What a jerk."

Josh set his backpack down and started to dress. He saw Seamus and Finnegan in another part of the room, but Freya and Charlie weren't there. He asked Bess where they were.

"They're helping Clatter bring the flamethrowers up," she said. "He keeps a locker of them in one of the lower levels."

"Have you played here before?" Josh asked as he stepped into his Torcher uniform.

"Once," Bess answered. "It's a little creepy. Most of the rides are pretty much gone, but a couple of them are still standing. They don't work, of course, but it's still weird walking around inside of them. She looked at Josh. "Don't worry, though. It'll be fun."

A curtain at the rear of the room opened and Clatter entered, accompanied by Freya and Charlie. Each of them carried a bag and set it on the ground. Freya unzipped one of them and removed three flamethrowers. She opened the other two bags and removed five more.

"Josh!" Clatter said. As he walked over to greet Josh, his coat of keys jangled merrily. "Are you ready for your first big game?"

Josh nodded. "I think so," he answered. "Who are we playing for?"

Clatter wagged a finger. "We never discuss the wagerers," he said. "You let me worry about that. You just focus on playing a good game."

Charlie came over to stand by Josh. "How are you feeling?" she asked in a whisper.

"Pretty good," Josh said. "Last night was amazing."

Charlie grinned. "Didn't I tell you?" she said.

Josh looked at her. There was something funny about her eyes. They weren't quite focusing on him.

"Are you on it now?" he asked.

Charlie giggled. "Yeah," she said.

"I thought you only use it when you play the holo-game," said Josh.

"Sometimes I take it when we're playing for real," Charlie answered. "It's even more intense then."

Josh looked around to make sure no one was listening. "Can I have one?" he asked.

Charlie shook her head. "You're not used to it yet."

"Come on," Josh begged.

Charlie leaned in close. "Don't talk about it here," she said. "And no, you can't have any. It's too risky."

Josh groaned. "You're no fun," he said, only half joking.

"Hey, guys." Scrawl entered the tent, shaking water from his coat. "Sorry I'm late. The damn train got stuck."

Josh looked over at Stash, waiting for him to say something smart. But Stash just looked down and dropped a shell onto the floor. *He's afraid of Scrawl,* Josh thought with some satisfaction. *He just thinks he can bully me because I'm the new guy. Well, we'll see about that.*

"Never mind," Clatter said to Scrawl. "Just get your team together and meet at the starting point in fifteen minutes. You know what to do."

Scrawl glanced at his watch. "No problem," he said. "We'll be ready."

Clatter looked around at the rest of them. "In that case I wish you all good luck and happy hunting," he said.

When Clatter was gone, Scrawl called everyone together. As he laced up his boots, he went over the plan for the game.

"We're starting at the entrance to the funhouse," he said. "Two teams. First team is Seamus, Finnegan, Bess, and me. Second team is Freya, Charlie, Josh, and Stash."

Josh groaned silently. Why did he have to be on a team with Stash? But at least Charlie would be with him.

"There's a total of twelve z's running around this place," Scrawl continued. "That means we each get at least one kill. The other four are up for grabs. But nobody hog them," he added, looking meaningfully at Stash. "Everybody gets a chance at the bonuses. Got it?"

Stash looked away. "Got it," he muttered.

"That's all there is to it," Scrawl said as he stood up. He turned to Josh. "Did you study the manual?"

"Yep," Josh said.

"I hope you memorized the maps," said Scrawl. "You'll need them to play this field. It's got some tricky sections."

"I'm good to go," Josh assured him.

"Put this in your ear," said Scrawl as he handed Josh device the size of a small gumball. "It's a communicator. You'll be able to hear everyone else, and they'll hear you. Keep the chatter to a minimum. You can imagine what it's like if everyone talks at once."

Josh tucked the communicator into his left ear. It fit snugly, then expanded to fill the space. There was a slight tickling sound as something bonded with his skin. "This is biotechnology," he said, surprised. "I thought only the military used stuff like this."

Scrawl grinned. "Like I told you before, Clatter has connections," he said. "Let's go."

They left the freak-show tent and walked to the end of the arcade, where a dilapidated structure with **FUN HOUSE** written across the front stood with its doors yawning open. Scrawl went inside, and the rest of the team followed.

Scrawl checked his watch. "We should be starting right . . . about . . . now," he said as the now-familiar electronic woman's voice came through the communicator in Josh's ear.

"Torchers, prepare for play," it said.

In front of them, mirrored doors swung inward, revealing a staircase going down. "Use the lights on your torches," Scrawl reminded them as he led the way.

Josh turned on his light, which produced a thin but clear beam courtesy of the halogen bulb mounted above the flamethrower's barrel. He kept it pointed down as he followed Seamus into the stairwell.

At the bottom of the stairs Scrawl stopped. "Team one, we're going north," he said, indicating a long hallway off to his left. Team two, head south."

Scrawl and his team moved out, leaving Josh, Charlie, Freya, and Stash at the foot of the stairs.

"Listen up," Freya said. "I want this to be quick and clean. We make a sweep of our quadrant, we torch anything we see that isn't human, and we collect our pay." She looked at Josh and spoke in a low voice. "Remember, there are cameras monitoring us at all times. The customers want to see action, so make sure you're always on."

Josh nodded. He understood the rules. If they performed well, the customers made bigger bets and everyone made more money. But Josh wasn't concerned just about the money. He wanted to show that he could really play.

"My guess is that we're going to have a six-and-six," Freya said as they started to walk. "Clatter almost always divides them up equally."

That means two of us will get a bonus z, Josh thought. He hoped he got one. He also hoped Stash didn't.

The tunnel they were in suddenly curved to the left and opened up into a small room filled with machinery. Freya turned to Josh. "Do you know where we are?"

Josh pulled an image of the map from his memory, trying to recall all the different sites. "The merry-go-round," he said. "We're underneath it."

"Good job," Freya said. "And ahead of us through the door on the other side?"

Stash made a spitting sound. "What is this, kindergarten?" he said. "It's the bumper cars, then the Tilt-A-Whirl, then the flying swings."

"Actually, it's the Tilt-A-Whirl, *then* the bumper cars," Josh said without thinking.

"Josh is right," Freya said.

Stash grunted and spat on the floor. Josh avoided looking at him, but he knew what the other boy was probably thinking. He chided himself, *You should have just kept your mouth shut.*

A crackling sound filled Josh's ear, followed by Clatter's voice. "Team one has located and neutralized one target," he said.

"Damn!" Stash said, slamming his hand against a piece of machinery. "They get the first-kill bonus."

"Calm down," Charlie said.

"We could have had it if we weren't standing around here chatting like a bunch of girls," Stash said angrily.

"We need to make up some time," Freya said, ignoring him. "Split up. Charlie, you come with me. Stash, you and Josh check out what's going on topside."

"Topside?" Stash groaned. "Why do I have to go topside?"

"Because I said so. Now shut up and *go*!"

Charlie and Freya headed off to the other side of the room, while Stash started climbing a ladder that ran up the side of one wall. He didn't say a word to Josh, who followed him, wishing he were with anyone else.

At the top of the ladder Stash pushed against a hatch that swung up and over. Then he put his head through the hole, looked around, and climbed out. Josh emerged after him into a gloomy tent that covered a large merry-go-round. Rain pounded on the roof and dripped through holes in the rotting canvas. In the semidarkness Josh saw the animals of the carousel sitting silently, their painted eyes staring straight ahead.

Stash still said nothing as he walked around the edge of the merry-go-round. Josh decided to walk in the other direction. The carousel was large enough that after a few steps he could no longer see Stash. Instead he focused on the merry-go-round itself. A meatbag could easily hide among the carved horses, tigers, and rabbits.

A second later he heard a whooshing sound and the clatter of broken glass. Then he heard Stash yell in frustration. As Josh started toward the other side, a figure emerged from the carousel and hobbled toward the side of the tent, where a slit in the canvas created a kind of doorway.

Josh aimed his flamethrower at the zombie. "Target in sight!" he shouted, and pulled the trigger. Just as he did, a second figure came flying out from between two horses. Startled, Josh jerked to the side so the stream of fire from his thrower missed the zombie and narrowly avoided catching the second figure, which fell to the ground bellowing in pain. Josh realized, too late, that it was Stash.

"Torcher down!" he yelled, kneeling down beside Stash.

"Get the hell away from me!" Stash shouted, shoving Josh. "You fouled my kill, you stupid noob." He stood up and ran after the zombie, who had managed to leave the tent.

Josh got up, retrieved his flamethrower from where it had fallen, and looked around. He knew he should follow Stash, but he really didn't want to be anywhere near him right now. It would be better for him if he returned to the hallway and tried to find Freya and Charlie. But he knew it was foolish to leave a Torcher alone chasing a z, especially one that might be wounded. *Besides,* he thought, *maybe this is another test.*

He heard a crackling in his earpiece, then Freya's voice came through. "Josh, what's the situation?"

Josh hesitated. He wanted to say that Stash was injured, but since Stash had run off he wasn't sure that was true. And he didn't want Freya to think he was panicking.

"We sighted a z," he said. "Stash is in pursuit."

"Good," Freya said. "Then you know what to do."

The communicator went silent. Before he could talk himself out of it, Josh pushed through the opening in the tent and found himself outside. It was raining even harder now, and he could barely see anything. But off to his right he saw a black figure entering one of the attractions. It had to be Stash.

He made his way along the arcade until he came to the spot where Stash had disappeared. "Great," he said, looking at the ride. "The Tunnel of Love."

Sighing, he ran up the ramp to the start of the ride, where a bunch of little boats that carried riders through the tunnel were gathered. The water in the imitation stream had long ago dried up, but the rain had filled it halfway. As Josh made his way to the heart-shaped opening of the ride, the water sloshed around his feet.

Josh walked carefully down the track and through the entrance. The inside of the ride was a mess. Overturned boats blocked his path, and pieces of fallen timber lay across the floor, crushing whatever they'd fallen on. Holes in the roof let in even more rain, and it was almost impossible to see anything. Josh tried using the light on his flamethrower, but it did little to help. Fortunately the flamethrower itself remained lit even in the rain.

He saw no sign of Stash or the zombie. How could they have disappeared so quickly? As far as Josh could tell, he was alone.

"Stash," he whispered. "Stash, do you copy?"

There was a hissing in his communicator, but no answer from Stash or anyone else. All he heard was static. He tapped his ear. "Stash? Freya? Charlie?"

There was no answer. Either something was blocking transmissions between the communicators or his was malfunctioning. Again he wondered if perhaps he was being tested. Maybe they'd turned off his communicator on purpose to see what he would do without it.

He worked his way deeper into the tunnel, becoming more and more certain that he had made a mistake. Stash had probably looked inside, seen no sign of the z, and left. Most likely he was looking for Josh right now and getting madder and madder. *What a great first game,* Josh thought miserably.

Then a loud creaking broke the silence, and a boat came rolling backward out of the rainy darkness toward Josh. He had to scramble sideways to avoid being hit, and just barely managed to get on the narrow walkway beside the track before the boat slid by him. It crashed into the stationary boat behind it, and Josh saw that it wasn't empty. Stash was in it, and he was being pushed over the edge by a zombie.

The zombie was a clown. Its face was painted white, with blue stars around its eyes and a big red mouth that grinned stupidly. It was wearing a red and white polka-dot suit with giant pom-pom buttons down the front, and its bushy pink hair stuck out like a cloud around its head. It had its hands around Stash's throat, and its face was hanging over his. Stash struggled, but he couldn't scream because he was being choked. Instead he writhed like a bug stuck on the end of a pin.

Josh readied his flamethrower but quickly realized there was no way he could use it without hitting Stash. Thinking quickly, he dropped the weapon on the walkway and rushed the boat. Jumping into it, he grabbed the zombie around the chest and wrenched it off Stash. The z hissed angrily and clawed at Josh's hands.

"Stash! Run!" Josh yelled.

Josh twisted to the side, still clutching the clown, and fell out of the boat. The zombie hit the floor first, with Josh on top of it. Scurrying back, Josh grabbed the barrel of the flamethrower and swung it up to firing position. He found the trigger and pulled, and the z burst into flame. To Josh's surprise, the zombie rolled over and over, trying to put the fire out. He'd never seen a meatbag do that before. Usually they just beat at the flames uselessly. This one seemed to be trying to save itself. But it was doomed.

Having taken care of the zombie, Josh rushed to the boat to make sure Stash was all right. He was sitting up, but he was holding his hand to his shoulder. "The damn thing bit me," he said, wincing in pain.

Bit? Josh thought. *Since when can animatronic zombies actually bite?* Before he could say anything, several figures emerged from the tunnel behind him. He whirled around, his flamethrower aimed at chest level.

"Weapon down!" he heard Scrawl shout.

Josh lowered the flamethrower. Scrawl jumped into the boat and took a look at Stash. Behind him, Seamus and Finnegan exchanged glances.

"I'm okay," Stash said weakly.

"You're bit," Scrawl said. "It's game over. You know the rules."

Stash began swearing, but he didn't argue. Scrawl turned to Josh. "That was a big risk you took," he said. "That z could easily have gotten you too."

Josh couldn't decide whether Scrawl was angry or not. He shrugged. "Stash needed help," he said.

Scrawl looked back at the injured player. "Yeah," he said. "He needs help."

"What happens now?" Josh asked. "Do we keep playing?"

"You do," Scrawl said. "We'll get Stash out of here. You meet up with the rest of the team. They're at the roller coaster. You know where it is?"

Josh nodded. "You're sure you don't need help with him?"

Scrawl shook his head. "We're good," he said. "You go. And hey, congrats on your first kill."

In all the commotion, Josh had forgotten about the zombie. He looked over at the smoking mess on the floor. "Thanks," he said.

12

Peering into the terrarium on Charlie's desk, Josh watched as the mechaspider spun its web. Its delicate body moved from side to side as the silk played out from its spinnerets. The mechaspider's intricately jointed legs moved in a slow ballet as the creature made its way around its web, spiraling out from the center and connecting to the glass walls of its enclosure.

"Isn't it beautiful?" Charlie said. "It's a golden orb weaver."

"It's really pretty," Josh agreed. The spider's oblong body shimmered in browns and golds, while its long legs were banded in black. A pattern of small white dots speckled its carapace.

"If it were real, I would feed it moths and bees," Charlie said.

"Have you ever seen a real one?" Josh asked her.

Charlie shook her head. "Biologists are supposedly growing them in labs from frozen eggs, but it will be a long time before most of us see real ones." She sighed. "Yet one more thing our ancestors ruined."

"My parents won't let us have any mechapets," Josh said. "My mother is freaked out by them."

Charlie laughed. "But doesn't she make imaginary animals real?" she said.

Josh laughed too. "I know. It's weird, right? But she says that at least those are real animals."

"I'm saving up for a tarantula," Charlie told him. "I know exactly which one I want. *Avicularia avicularia,* the Guyana pinktoe."

"Pinktoe?" said Josh. "That doesn't sound very spidery."

Charlie shook her head. "You should see them," she said. "They're all black except for the ends of their feet, which are pink. They live in trees and never touch the ground. That's what I like about them. They're always looking down on the world." She smiled. "I have almost enough to get one," she said. "Two more kills and it's mine."

Josh walked away from the spider terrarium and stood at one of the windows, looking out at the street. It was Sunday afternoon. This time he'd told his parents he was going out to take pictures for a photography-class project. He felt bad about lying to them again—particularly when they'd told him to have a good time—but he'd really needed to talk to Charlie.

"How's Stash doing?" he asked. It was still raining. A woman was walking by, holding the hand of a small child in a red raincoat. The woman was trying to cover them both with an umbrella, but the child wanted to walk in the rain and was pulling on the woman's arm and laughing.

"I guess he's fine," Charlie answered. "Clatter was fixing him up."

"Do people get bit often?"

"Not often," said Charlie. "But sometimes."

"Have you?" Josh asked her.

Charlie shook her head. "No," she said. "And I don't want to. The meatbags may not be real, but they can do some damage."

Josh had been thinking about what had happened, and it bothered him a little bit that Clatter's cyber-zombies could really hurt the players. Torching the meatbags was one thing. They couldn't feel pain. But Josh and the other players could, and putting them in danger like that seemed . . . strange. "Don't you worry about getting hurt?"

"It's all part of the game," said Charlie. "The

wagerers like it to be realistic."

That made sense to Josh. After all, they were paying big money. The more real the game seemed, the more interested they would be. And ultimately he benefited. He thought about the money sitting in the box in his closet. He'd been shocked at how much Clatter had given him at the end of the game. It was more money than he'd ever had.

"You were lucky to get that bonus," Charlie said. "If I'd been a little quicker on the draw, it would have been mine."

The woman and the child turned the corner and disappeared. Josh looked at Charlie, who was now lying on her back on her bed, her head hanging over the side. "Sorry," Josh said. "I didn't mean to steal it."

"It's okay," said Charlie. "I'm just teasing. You played a great game. It wouldn't surprise me if clients started betting on you."

Josh felt a swell of pride at the thought that after only a couple of games he might be one of the favorite players.

"That's what you really want," said Charlie, sitting up. "Then, on top of bonuses, you get a bigger cut. Scrawl gets something like twenty percent of everything people bet on him."

Josh whistled. "That's impressive," he said.

"I'm up to ten percent," Charlie informed him. "I bet you'll be there soon. Clatter likes you."

Josh turned around. "I'm having a blast," he said. "Thanks again for recruiting me."

"Thank *you*," Charlie said. "Clatter was so impressed by your game that he gave me a bonus for finding you."

Josh gave her a stern look. "And you're not giving me half?" he said, pretending to be angry.

Charlie laughed. "No way," she said. "That's one eighth of a mechaspider. It's all mine. Besides," she added, "I told you about Z. You can consider that your bonus."

"That stuff is intense," he said.

"It's great, isn't it?" Charlie said. "Wait until you try playing a game while you're on it. It's like you and the z's are connected. You find them a lot faster."

Josh cleared his throat. "Where can I get some?" he asked, trying to sound casual.

Charlie sat up. "You're in luck," she said. "I think I can spare a couple." She got up and went to her dresser, returning with the silver vial. Unscrewing the lid, she poured half a dozen tablets into her hand, which she held out toward Josh.

Josh walked over to her and reached for the pills. As his fingers came near them, Charlie made a fist, hiding the Z from him. "I didn't say they were free," she said.

Josh looked at her. "How much?" he asked.

Charlie's dark eyes sparkled. "It'll cost you a kiss," she said.

Josh hesitated. Was she kidding? He looked at her closed fist, then back at her face. She was staring him straight in the eye, not blinking. Slowly he leaned toward her. He saw her close her eyes and open her mouth. His lips touched hers. Her mouth was soft. He kissed her quickly and pulled away.

Charlie opened her eyes and lifted one eyebrow. "I think that was worth one," she said. She opened her fist and handed Josh one pill. "How many more do you want?"

Josh kissed her again. This time he lingered longer. He felt her arms go around him, the fist holding the Z pressing against his back.

When he finally pulled away, Josh felt himself blushing. Charlie smiled. "Okay," she said. "I think that one is good for the rest of these." She tucked the Z into his hand and closed his fingers over the pills.

"Um, I don't want you to think that these are the only reason I did that," Josh told her as he put them in his pocket.

"Oh, I know," Charlie said. "I figured you just

needed a little incentive."

Josh looked down. "Okay, then," he said, not knowing what else to say.

"Besides, now Bess owes me twenty bucks," Charlie said.

Josh looked up. "She bet you I wouldn't kiss you?" he said.

"It was a sucker bet," said Charlie. "I knew you'd do it."

Josh didn't know whether to laugh or be offended. "I can't believe you bet on me!" he said.

"I *said* I knew you would do it," Charlie reminded him. "It wasn't much of a bet. Come on. Let's get something to eat."

They went down the stairs. But as they entered the second-floor workspace, Charlie suddenly stopped. A man was standing in the middle of the room, a welding torch in his hand. He turned and looked at them, and Josh saw that one half of his face was badly burned. The skin there was thickly scarred, and his eye was missing.

"Dad," Charlie said.

The man's eye moved to Josh, then back to his daughter. "Who's he?" he asked.

Charlie didn't answer. She seemed to be frozen.

"Josh," Josh said. "It's nice to meet you."

The man grunted in reply.

"I didn't hear you come in," Charlie said quietly.

"Is he one of your Torcher friends?" her father asked.

Charlie shook her head. "We have a class together," she said. "We were just doing homework."

Her father looked at Josh again but didn't say anything. He turned back to the sculpture he was working on and began welding a piece of metal to one of the outstretched arms. A hand had formed, and he was adding a finger to it.

"Let's go," Charlie whispered to Josh. They skirted the room, avoiding her father, and went downstairs.

"I'm sorry about that," Charlie said when they were out on the street. The rain had slowed to a drizzle, and they walked through the puddles left behind.

"It's okay," Josh assured her. "He seems . . ." He looked for a word to finish his sentence.

"You don't have to say anything," said Charlie.

Josh reached out and took her hand, and she let him. "What happened to him?" he asked.

He felt Charlie stiffen.

"He got bit," she said.

"By a z?" Josh asked, shocked.

"Yeah," Charlie replied.

"Then shouldn't he be—"

"Dead," Charlie said. "Yeah. He should be. But when he was bit, he torched himself. He burned the bite."

Josh couldn't believe it. "He burned his own face?" he asked.

"It killed the virus before it could infect him," Charlie said. "They weren't sure that it had really worked, so they kept him in quarantine for six months. When he didn't show any signs of turning, they let him out."

Josh tried to imagine what it would be like to torch his own face. There was no way he could do it.

"That's why he doesn't want me playing the game," said Charlie.

"He knows about—" Josh began.

"No," Charlie interrupted him. "Not about the real game. He thinks I only play the hologame. If he knew about the real game, I don't know what he would do."

"Well, I think I can handle being your study buddy," Josh joked.

They walked in silence for a minute. Then Charlie spoke. "I told you my mother was dead," Charlie said. "That's not true. She couldn't handle it when my father came home. They fought all the time and finally she left. I don't know where she is."

"But how could she leave you behind?" Josh asked before he could stop himself. "I mean . . . sorry."

"It wasn't all her fault," Charlie said. "My dad was really angry. Violent. But he was never bad to me," she added. "Never. My mother said I was the only one who could take care of him."

"And you don't know where she is?"

"No. It's better this way," Charlie answered.

Josh wanted to ask her how it could possibly be better, but he didn't.

"I'm sorry I lied to you," Charlie said. "About my family being normal. Remember, I told you we were the only ones on the team with boring stories."

Josh chuckled. "Oh yeah," he said.

He saw a tear slip from Charlie's eye.

"Don't start crying on me," he said.

"I'm not crying," Charlie objected. "It's the rain."

"Okay, then," said Josh. "Because I'm pretty sure that's the Seventh Rule of Torching: No crying."

Charlie laughed as she wiped her eye. "That must be in the revised edition," she said. "I'll try to remember that."

"You'd better," said Josh as they continued to walk. "You never know when there will be a pop quiz."

13

On Monday Josh was at his locker, hanging up his coat, when Firecracker appeared. "Where were you yesterday?" he asked.

Josh shut his locker. "Why?" he said. He hadn't spoken to Firecracker since the incident with their report, and things were still a little weird between them. In addition, he had a headache. He'd taken a Z the night before and spent almost all night playing the hologame with Charlie.

"I called," Firecracker said. "Your dad said you were out taking pictures."

"So?" said Josh.

Firecracker snorted. "Come on," he said. "What do you think I am, stupid?"

"You said it, not me," Josh snapped. He started to walk away.

"Hey!" Firecracker called after him. "What's your problem?"

Josh ignored him. He wasn't in the mood to talk to Firecracker. Last night he'd played a zombie for the first time in the hologame. Now he understood why Charlie liked it. The Z had really helped him get into the zombie mood. He'd seen things differently, felt things differently. Everything had been more intense—primal. He'd hunted the Torchers like they were animals, smelling them out and following the sound of their hearts beating. He'd killed four of them and gained sixteen experience levels.

But the Z had also kept him up all night, and now he was exhausted. He thought about taking half a Z this morning, but he didn't want to waste it. They had practice that afternoon, and he wanted to save it for that.

Josh managed to avoid Firecracker the rest of day, though it meant skipping lunch and hiding out in the bathroom. But that was okay—it gave him some time to rest. He'd actually fallen asleep in the bathroom stall, waking up only when some seniors dragged a freshman into the bathroom and threatened to dunk his head in the toilet if he didn't pay them off. The kid had screamed bloody murder, and Josh jolted awake thinking he was in the middle of a game.

Now the day was over and he was on the train heading to the Docklands. He couldn't wait to see Charlie and to play with the rest of the team. He also wanted to find out if Stash was okay. He didn't like the guy, but he was still a Torcher, and they had to look out for one another.

When he reached his stop, he got off and walked toward the wharf. He was thinking about the Z in his pocket, and not really watching where he was going. So when someone came up from behind and grabbed his arm, he yelled in surprise.

"It's just me," Firecracker said, holding his hands up.

Josh stared at him. "Are you following me?" he asked.

"I just want to talk," Firecracker said. "What's up with you?"

"Nothing's *up* with me," said Josh.

"Then what are you doing in the Docklands? Coming to help the homeless?" Firecracker stared at Josh, daring him to lie.

"It's none of your business," said Josh. "Just go home."

"Or what?" Firecracker asked.

Josh felt himself getting angry. "Just go," he said. "Leave me alone."

He turned and started to walk away, hoping that Firecracker would give up and go the other way. No such luck. Firecracker rushed forward to block Josh's path. "I want to know what you're doing," he said.

Josh stared at his friend. Why couldn't Firecracker just let it go? He started to push past, but Firecracker moved over and cut him off.

Without thinking, Josh shoved him. Firecracker reeled backward but didn't fall. His face reddened and he stormed toward Josh. The two collided, Firecracker pushing Josh against a brick wall. Two Zooeys who had been standing on the corner turned to stare at them.

"Get off!" Josh grunted, trying to push Firecracker away.

"Josh, come *on*," said Firecracker. "Tell me what's going on."

Josh put one foot against the wall and used it to push himself forward. Firecracker stumbled back. Caught off balance, he was an easy target. Josh punched him in the stomach, and Firecracker crumpled to his knees.

"Hey!" yelled one of the Zooeys, a boy in a duck costume. "Fighting isn't cool!"

Josh took a few steps toward the boy and the other Zooey, a girl dressed like a koala bear, grabbed the duck's hand and pulled him away. Josh turned back to Firecracker, who was standing up again, holding his stomach.

Before Josh could react, Firecracker swung at him. His fist connected with Josh's cheek, and there was a sharp crack. Pain exploded in Josh's head. He ran at Firecracker, tackling him. The two of them fell to the sidewalk, where they wrestled for position until finally Josh had Firecracker pinned beneath him.

"Get it through your thick head," Josh said, flecking Firecracker's face with spittle. "I don't want you following me."

He could see confusion in Firecracker's eyes, and for a moment he felt bad and almost broke down and told the truth. Then he remembered that if he let Firecracker know what was going on, he would be risking everything. He had to keep his part in the game a secret.

"Stay away," he said. "You got that?"

He waited for Firecracker to nod, then got up. Without looking back, he walked as quickly as he could down the street. He turned a corner and waited to see if Firecracker passed him. After a minute he took a look and saw that the sidewalk was empty. *He's gone,* he thought with relief.

Still, he took a different route to the shipyard. He didn't want to take any chances. Firecracker *wasn't* stupid. He was a good tracker, and he could easily be tailing Josh. But Josh was pretty sure he had hurt

Firecracker's pride enough that he would just leave. He hated himself for having done that to his best friend, but he'd had to—for both their sakes.

Only when he was safely in the tunnel walking to the ship graveyard did he relax a little bit. He was all right. Firecracker didn't know anything.

When he saw Charlie sitting on top of a ship's propeller, cleaning her flamethrower, he felt much better. She saw him and waved. "Hey there," she said. "I've been waiting for you."

"Yeah?" Josh said. "Why's that?"

"So I could give you this," Charlie answered, giving him a quick kiss. Josh tried for another one, but Charlie shook her head. "We have to be careful," she said. "Team romances are kind of a no-no."

Josh sighed. "I suppose I can do that," he said dramatically. Then he pretended to think of something. "*Or* I could break up with you. Then it wouldn't be a problem."

"Just *try* breaking it off," said Charlie, squinting. "Then next time you've got a z after you, I might just have to trip you."

Josh didn't say anything, distracted by the throbbing in his cheek.

"Come on. I'm just joking. Don't be mad."

"It's not that," said Josh. He hesitated, not sure

he should tell Charlie what had happened. Then he sighed. "It's Firecracker. He followed me today."

Charlie's eyes widened. "He followed you? Did he see where you went?"

"No. I caught him in time," Josh answered.

"Don't tell Clatter," Charlie said quickly. "He's super paranoid about that kind of thing. Keep it to yourself."

"All right," said Josh. "I'm going to get changed."

He left her to finish cleaning her thrower and went to the locker room. Finnegan, Seamus, and Scrawl were already there, talking, but when Josh came in they stopped abruptly.

"Hey," Josh said. "Am I interrupting something?"

Finnegan and Seamus didn't say anything, but Scrawl shook his head. "Nah," he said. "We were just talking about Stash."

"How is he?" Josh asked as he opened his locker and took his uniform out.

"Not great," Scrawl said. "He'll be fine, but his bite got infected and he won't be playing for a while."

Josh slipped into his uniform. "How does a cyber-bite get infected?" he asked.

He saw Seamus and Finnegan look at each other. Then Finnegan said, "He got dirt in it. We told him to be careful, but you know Stash."

Josh snorted. "Yeah," he said. When nobody responded, he added, "Not that he isn't a good guy, or anything."

"It's okay," Finnegan told him. "We all know Stash can be a jerk."

Josh smiled. "That doesn't mean I want him to get hurt," he said.

"Like I said, he'll be fine," Scrawl said. "He's just on temporary time out. Now let's go kick some zombie butt."

The others left the locker room, and Josh sat on the bench to tie his boots. Then he reached into the pocket of his jeans and took out half a tablet of Z. He put it in his mouth and swallowed hard, feeling it go down.

When he rejoined the group, they were still waiting for Freya, so everyone was just hanging out talking. Bess came up to Josh, frowning. "You cost me twenty bucks," she said, crossing her arms over her chest. "Charlie told me all about it," she whispered. Then she made kissing sounds with her lips.

Josh looked over at Charlie. She was looking up at the ceiling, pretending to be interested in something.

"I'm going to get both of you," Josh told Bess. "You just wait."

"Ooh, I'm scared," Bess said, wiggling her fingers and miming fear.

Josh walked over to Charlie. "I thought we weren't telling anyone," he said.

"I *had* to tell Bess," said Charlie. "Otherwise I would have owed *her* twenty bucks." She laughed.

"Hey," Charlie said, looking around. "Did you take the Z?"

Josh nodded.

"Me too," Charlie said. "Let's make sure we're on the same team for practice. We'll kill!"

Caught up in Charlie's excitement, Josh forgot all about Firecracker and his earlier worries. The Z was starting to work, and his thoughts were slipping away.

"Kill," he said, grinning at Charlie. "That's just what we'll do."

14

Josh looked down the stairs. Something was moving below him; there was a slight shifting of the shadows that normally he might not notice. But the Z had worked its magic on his brain, and although his thoughts were a little hazy, he was sensing things more acutely. He sniffed, smelling something dank.

"Water," he said.

Finnegan switched on his torch's light and shone it into the darkness. A dozen steps down, the stairs disappeared into water. "Good work, genius," Finnegan said.

Ever since Finnegan had been assigned to a team with Josh, Charlie, and Bess, he'd been acting weird. Assuming it was because he had been separated from his brother, Josh was trying not to let Finnegan's comments bother him. But his patience was wearing thin.

"What's your problem?" he demanded.

Finnegan stepped back. "I don't have a problem," he said, sounding surprised.

Josh grinned. "I didn't think so. So how about you go first down the stairs, then?"

Suddenly Charlie was beside him. "Ease up," she whispered so that only he could hear.

Josh laughed. "I'm fine," he said.

Charlie grabbed his elbow. "Josh," she said. "I'm serious. Just cool it, okay?"

Josh closed his eyes and took a few deep breaths, until he calmed down a little. "I'm fine," he told Charlie.

"Josh, you take lead," Bess said. "Finn, you're rear man."

Josh glared at Finnegan. "No problem," Josh said.

He descended quickly, moving faster than he knew he should. The light mounted on his flamethrower cut through the blackness. When he reached the point where the water met the stairs, he kept going, never hesitating. The cold water slid over his boots and up his legs, and still Josh didn't slow down.

When the water was up to his waist, the stairs ran out and he was on level ground. Ten feet ahead of him the opening to a huge pipe gaped like an open mouth about twelve feet across. The metal was rusted and flaking off, and the water was speckled with tiny pieces of it.

"What is this place?" Josh asked.

"One of the intake tunnels," said Bess. "This is where the water came in to flood the main room and raise the ships to the surface. There are a dozen of them." She shone her light at the top of the tunnel entrance, where a number was etched into the steel. "This is tunnel nine."

"The worst one," Finnegan mumbled.

"The *hardest* one," said Charlie, correcting him.

"Why?" Josh asked.

"This one is still live," Bess explained. "The others were turned off years ago, but this one still works. It's connected to a line used by the city to take water from the ocean to use in the hydrogenerators that power the subway. The guys who built this place tapped into that line. They installed a valve to open and close it, but when they abandoned it, that valve was stuck halfway open. So whenever the city uses this particular line, water comes through tunnel nine too."

"What she's trying to say is that this place can flood at any second," Finnegan added.

"Not any second," Charlie countered. "You get a warning, at least if you keep your ears open."

"Right," said Bess. "When water moves through the main line, you can hear it. Then you know you have about three minutes to get out of the tunnel before it starts filling up."

"What kind of noise?" Josh asked her.

"It's hard to explain," Bess answered. "Trust me, you'll know it when you hear it."

"How often do they use the line?"

"Not often," said Charlie. "The lines are old, so they rotate between them. This one gets used maybe three times a month."

"But never on the same day," Finnegan added.

Josh looked at the water. "It looks like they've used it pretty recently," he remarked. "Look how high it is."

Bess shook her head. "It's always at least this high," she said. "Remember, the valve is stuck halfway open. When the tunnel floods, it only drains back out to the level of the valve opening."

"Why not just fix the valve?"

"Clatter thinks it makes a great training zone," Charlie said.

"And he's right," said Bess.

"Wait a minute," Josh said. "If the tunnel goes straight in and straight out, what's the big deal? We just go in until we find the z's, torch them, and get out."

Finnegan laughed but said nothing.

"It's not that easy," Charlie said. "The tunnel

doesn't just run straight through. It's in five sections, with a flood chamber between each section and the next. The flood chambers have a hatch door on each side. If the tunnel starts to flood, theoretically you can release the door closest to the main line and prevent the water from coming any farther this way."

"Theoretically?" said Josh.

"They don't always work," Finnegan said. "The machinery is old. Some of it is broken. Some of it sticks. You just never know."

"Each flood chamber has a shaft that runs up to the surface," Bess continued. "It's a way to vent water if it builds up. There's also a ladder in each shaft, kind of an escape route if you're trapped in the room."

"Not that you're likely to make it," said Finnegan. "More than likely the water will rise faster than you can climb."

"There are also some smaller access tunnels," Charlie said. "They link the twelve tunnels together. But they're really only wide enough to crawl through."

"Which the z's are really good at," said Finnegan.

Josh tried to make sense of everything he was being told. Normally it wouldn't be a problem, but the Z was making it hard to analyze everything clearly. *Hatches*, he thought. *Access tunnels. Flood chambers.*

Individually the words made sense, but when he tried to put them all together, things got a little fuzzy.

"So you're saying that the z's could be anywhere," he said finally. "Got it. Let's go torching."

Without waiting for the others, he pushed ahead through the water. His eyes quickly adapted to the darkness, another benefit of taking the Z. He watched the shadows carefully for signs of movement but saw nothing.

After about a hundred yards they came to a wall that prevented them from going forward. A circular door about six feet across and made of thick steel was set into the center of the wall.

"This is the first hatch door," Bess said, shining her light on the door. "See that lever on the right?"

Josh looked where her beam was pointing and saw a rectangular box about a foot high affixed to the wall beside the door. A metal rod extended from it at an angle.

"When you pull the lever, it activates the chains that raise and lower the door," said Bess. She reached for it. "Be ready to shoot if there's anything inside."

Josh and the others stood back, their flamethrowers held out in front of them, as Bess pulled the rod down. There was a grinding sound as the heavy door rose straight up into the ceiling.

Josh stepped through the opening and found himself in a square chamber approximately fifteen feet on each side. From the doorway, steps led down from the tunnel to the room's floor. On the opposite side of the room another set of steps went up to a hatch door that was partially open. The room was filled with water that left only three steps exposed.

"Doesn't look like there are any meatbags in here," said Josh, shining his light around. He walked down the steps and into the partially flooded chamber. When his feet touched the floor, the water was just above his waist. As he waded across the room, he noticed a ladder affixed to the wall on his left. It led to a hole in the ceiling, and he guessed it was the escape shaft Bess had mentioned.

"Where are the access tunnels you talked about?" he asked Bess. "I don't see any other ways in or out."

"They're below water level right now," Bess said. "It's different in each room. You just have to look everywhere."

They made their way to the other side of the chamber and ducked beneath the partially opened hatch door to reenter the tunnel. The next stretch was as empty as the first, and Josh found himself getting bored.

"The other team better not get all the z's," he complained.

"Don't worry," Finnegan said. "You'll get your share."

When they reached the second chamber and found it empty, Josh was annoyed. "This is a waste of time," he said as he surveyed the room. "We might as well go back."

All of a sudden a loud clanking sound filled the room, and the hatch door behind them crashed closed, falling from the ceiling as the chains rattled violently. They all swirled around and stared at it.

"How did that happen?" Bess yelled. She looked at Finnegan, who was standing closest to the control box, but he shook his head.

"It wasn't me," he said, showing her that he was holding his flamethrower with both hands.

"Somebody had to have touched something," Bess insisted. "The hatches don't just—"

She was cut off as the water exploded upward. Three zombies rose from the bottom, screeching as they clawed at the air.

"Meatbags!" Josh yelled. "Torch them!"

One of the zombies—a man in a tattered suit— lunged at Josh. With no room to use his flamethrower, Josh used it as a club instead, butting the man in the chest with it so that he staggered back and fell into the water.

The other two zombies—an old woman with gray hair and a boy in a scouting uniform—were trying to get up the stairs to where Finnegan was standing. He aimed his flamethrower at them and pulled the trigger. The two z's burst into flame, but Charlie had to dive sideways to avoid being hit as well. When she came up she was sputtering.

"Finnegan, you idiot!" she yelled as the flaming zombies swirled around her.

The man who had attacked Josh was back on his feet. This time Josh did flame him, but even on fire he kept coming. In fact, the three z's had somehow managed to get between the four Torchers and the tunnel door.

"This way!" Finnegan yelled, sloshing through the water toward the opposite door.

The four of them made it into the next section of tunnel as the burning zombies stumbled after them. One of them—the scout—fell into the water, causing a cloud of hissing steam to rise around him. The other two continued on, moaning.

"Out of the way!" Charlie shouted, pulling on the lever sticking from the hatch-door control box.

Nothing happened. Charlie pulled again. There was a grinding sound, as if the gears were trying to work, but still the door didn't budge.

"Keep going," Bess ordered, turning and heading further into the tunnel.

"What about the z's?" Josh asked as they jogged along.

"They'll burn out," said Bess. "Don't worry about them. Worry about the ones we can't see."

"It's like they were *herding* us," said Charlie. "Like they'd set a trap to get us to go this way."

"Please," Finnegan sneered. "They're not that smart. They're not *any* kind of smart."

"Then who shut the hatch door?" Charlie snapped back.

"It was an accident," said Finnegan.

"Whatever it was, we can't go back that way," Bess reminded them. "We'll have to use one of the escape shafts."

"We've never done that," said Charlie.

"There's a first time for everything," Bess said, grinning.

Josh's head ached. His sense of smell had grown stronger, and the odors of rusting steel, stagnant water, and now the stench of the burning zombies filled his nose. His heart was beating more quickly, and there was a ringing in his ears.

They burst into the third chamber, which was empty like the first.

"I don't like this," said Finnegan as they waded through the room. "I *really* don't like this. We should go back."

"Not until we complete the mission," Bess insisted. "There's one more chamber and then the final part of the tunnel. Then we're out of here."

They were halfway down the fourth length of tunnel when they heard the grating of metal on metal behind them. Finnegan, turning around, shone his light into the darkness. The beam illuminated a shut hatch door.

Finnegan ran toward the door. "Who did that?" he shouted.

"Finnegan! Get back here!" Bess's voice was forceful, but Josh sensed fear in it as well.

Finnegan stopped and stared at the hatch door for a moment before going to the control lever and pulling it. Nothing happened. When Finnegan turned around, his face was a mask of panic.

"Now do you think they aren't smart enough?" Charlie asked.

Finnegan walked back to them, shaking his head. "No," he said. "There's no way. They can't do this."

Josh heard himself laugh. "What are you guys afraid of?" he said. "They're just cybots. You're acting like they're really trying to kill us."

For a moment he thought he saw Finnegan and Bess exchange a look, then Bess was all business. "Josh is right. But we still want to complete the mission. The fourth flood chamber is up ahead. We'll sweep it, check out the tunnel beyond it, and finish up. I'm sure Clatter set this all up to test us. Nobody panic, all right?"

Charlie and Finnegan nodded. Josh laughed again. Despite the situation, he felt powerful. Or was he laughing at the others because he was thinking like a z? He didn't know, and he didn't care. He was having a great time.

They kept moving. In the fourth chamber they found a single zombie. Dressed in overalls, it was just wandering around holding a wrench in its hand. Charlie torched it without any trouble.

As they headed up the steps to the final length of tunnel, Finnegan stopped. "Maybe one of us should wait here," he said.

Josh turned around. "Why?"

"The hatch got shut after we left the chamber," Finnegan reminded him. "If one of us stays here, we can at least make sure no one messes with it from this side."

"That's a good point," Bess agreed. "You stay here. The three of us will go on."

"He's afraid," Josh said to Charlie as they walked into the tunnel.

Charlie nudged him with her elbow. "Don't make fun of him," she said, but Josh heard her giggle.

"Oh no!" Josh said, imitating Finnegan's voice. "A zombie! Seamus, help me!"

Again Charlie giggled, but this time Bess turned around and shushed them. "Keep it down," she ordered. "You never know when—"

A sudden rumbling interrupted her. The tunnel shook slightly, making the water slosh from side to side.

"The main line!" Charlie yelped. "It's filling up!"

"Go!" said Bess, pushing them. "Back to the flood chamber!"

Josh stumbled as he tried to run through the water. It seemed to be pulling at him, holding him back. Behind him he heard a low growling.

"The water is coming," said Charlie. "Hurry!"

They reached the chamber, where they found Finnegan standing on the steps. "Is it the main?" he asked.

"Get the hatch shut!" Bess barked. "That will stop it."

Finnegan grabbed the lever and pulled. It broke off in his hand, leaving just a stub of metal. He looked at it helplessly. Josh ran over and pushed him out of the way. Grabbing the short length of metal, he pulled as hard as he could. The jagged end of the broken lever cut into his palm, and blood ran down his wrist. The lever didn't move.

"There's no time," said Bess. "And we can't get back to the third chamber. We have to go up."

As she spoke, more water surged in through the tunnel. Finnegan let out a frightened squeak and ran for the ladder affixed to the wall beside the open hatch door. He dropped his flamethrower and started climbing, ignoring the rest of them. Josh watched his head disappear into the hole in the ceiling.

"Does he know where he's going?" he asked Bess.

"None of us do," Bess said. "Just go. We'll figure it out."

Josh waited for Charlie to start up the ladder, then motioned for Bess to follow her. Bess shook her head. "I'm the team leader," she said. "I go last. And don't argue. We don't have time."

Josh looked at the water, which was rising more quickly than he thought it would. Already the steps were covered, and even as he watched it rose another inch.

He slung his flamethrower over his shoulder and started up the ladder, ignoring the pain in his wounded hand. Ahead of him Charlie was passing through the hole in the ceiling. Josh wondered what was waiting for them there.

He found out a moment later when he emerged into a small space. Instead of going up further, as he'd expected it to, the ladder ended there, and another tunnel continued off to the left. Charlie was moving through it on her hands and knees.

Josh heard Bess come up behind him. "What's the holdup?" she shouted. "This place is about to turn into a swimming pool."

Josh moved as quickly as he could, sliding into the tunnel. He heard Bess start to follow him. Then she yelped in surprise.

"A z has me!" she called to Josh.

Unable to turn around in the tunnel, Josh bowed his head and tried to look through his legs. He saw Bess's startled face for a moment, illuminated by the light of her flamethrower. Then she was pulled backward.

"Josh!" she cried.

Josh heard the mumbled moaning of a z. It was dragging Bess back to the hole in the ceiling.

"Kick!" Josh shouted.

"I'm trying!" Bess shouted back. "It won't let go!"

Josh didn't know what to do. He couldn't turn

around. He couldn't maneuver his flamethrower in the small space. Even if he could get to it, he couldn't shoot past Bess.

He could hear Bess ramming her foot into the z. She was also shouting at it to let go. Josh looked ahead. Somewhere in the darkness Charlie and Finnegan were still crawling. Calling to them wouldn't help, though—they couldn't turn around either.

It was up to him.

Just as he was trying to formulate a plan he felt something wet against his knees. *Water,* he thought vaguely. *Water is coming in.*

Behind him Bess choked. Then she screamed. "It bit me!" she yelled.

The water was coming in more quickly now. Josh realized that the flood chamber must have filled up and the water was being forced into the tunnel. But surely *someone* must know they were trapped in there, and would somehow reroute the water. They wouldn't just be allowed to die.

"Josh! Go!" Bess called out. She choked again. "My body will block some of the water, but not for long."

"I'm not just leaving you here!" Josh yelled.

"I'm bit," said Bess, her voice softer now. "Just leave me."

"It's a *game!*" Josh said, becoming more frantic as

the water rose past his hands. "The bite doesn't matter. But if you don't move *now*, you're going to drown."

"Josh, listen to me." Bess's voice was eerily calm. "I'm the squad leader, and I'm telling you to go."

Josh started to argue, but something in Bess's voice told him not to. Besides, his survival instinct was screaming at him to move. "I'll get help," he told Bess. "We'll be back."

He crawled forward as quickly as he could. The rough metal scraped his palms raw, and he could feel the water rising quickly. It was almost up to his chest now, and in another minute or two he wouldn't be able to breathe. He tried not to think about Bess. *It's going to be all right,* he told himself, repeating it over and over as he scrambled through the black tunnel.

The tunnel seemed to go on forever. Then it opened up into a square shaft maybe three feet on each side. The shaft rose straight up, a ladder attached to one wall. Above him Josh saw a tiny point of light.

"Charlie?" he yelled. "Charlie, is that you?"

"Josh!" Charlie's voice echoed down the shaft. "Hurry! There's a tunnel up here that we think leads back to the surface."

The water pouring into the shaft was filling it up quickly. Josh grabbed the ladder and started climbing, staying just a few steps ahead of the water. When he reached the top, he saw Charlie.

"Come on!" Charlie yelled, grabbing his hand. "Where's Bess?"

Josh shook his head. Charlie froze, horror crossing her face. Then Finnegan yelled at them to hurry, and she moved. Josh followed as they ran through yet another tunnel, this one built out of brick.

"How do you know this takes us back to the surface?" Josh asked as they ran.

"There was a diagram on the wall back there," said Finnegan. "Right up here should be a set of stairs."

Moments later the stairs came into view. But blocking them was a z, a big man whose muscled body was bleeding from multiple wounds, as if he'd been tearing at his own skin. Seeing the three Torchers, he lurched toward them.

Barely thinking, Josh rushed at the zombie, tackling him and pushing him against the wall.

"Josh!" Charlie shouted. "The blood! Don't touch it! Your hands are cut!"

Who cares about fake blood? Josh thought as he fought the zombie, who was thrashing his head from side to side and trying to bite Josh's face.

He saw Finnegan run by him and up the stairs. Charlie was next. As she passed Josh, she grabbed his arm and pulled. "Come on!" she said.

Josh was staring into the zombie's rheumy eyes. It was gnashing its teeth, or what was left of them, and its tongue was lolling from its mouth. Blood and spittle flecked its chin. It was disgusting, but for some reason Josh couldn't stop looking at it. His brain slowed down, as if he and the zombie were thinking the same thoughts.

Then Charlie yanked hard on his arm and tore him away. She practically dragged him up the first dozen steps before pushing him behind her and raising her flamethrower. Josh watched as she shot a blast of fire at the z, which was trying to climb the stairs after them. Charlie kept the flame burning for longer than usual, and when she released the trigger, the zombie's skin was blackened, falling to the stone steps in bloody chunks.

"That's for Bess," Charlie whispered. Then she turned around and took Josh's hand, and they started to climb.

15

The tap on his shoulder startled Josh. He jumped and opened his eyes. Emily was standing beside his bed, looking at him curiously. Josh removed the headset he was wearing and turned it off.

"Sorry," Emily said. "I knocked, but you didn't hear me. What are you listening to?"

"Crystal Static," said Josh. "What do you want?"

Emily frowned. "What's your problem?" she asked. "You've been grumpy ever since you got home. Did one of the homeless people make fun of your clothes or something?"

"You know how Mondays can be," Josh answered. He wasn't about to tell her that he was upset because Bess had almost died in the game that afternoon. He still couldn't believe Clatter, Scrawl, and Seamus had managed to get into the sealed chamber through the tunnel and get her out. By the time he, Charlie, and Finnegan had reached the surface, Bess had been transported to the hospital, where she was recovering.

Clatter had apologized repeatedly for the mechanical malfunctions he said caused the hatch doors to lock, and Josh knew he felt terrible about the accident. He'd praised Josh for his quick thinking under pressure. But even knowing that Bess was alive couldn't help Josh shake the memory of seeing her face for what he thought was the last time. She'd looked so scared, and he'd had to leave her there alone to—he thought—die.

He shook the thoughts from his head and looked at Emily. "So what do you want?"

"I'm having trouble with my homework," said Emily. "I was wondering if you could help me."

"Can't you ask Mom or Dad?"

"I could," said Emily. "But I don't want to. Besides, they're busy."

"So am I," Josh told her.

"Busy doing nothing," said Emily. "You've been 'busy' for two weeks."

"I have a lot to do," Josh said. "You wouldn't understand."

"You mean your new girlfriend?" said Emily.

Josh sat up. "What are you talking about?"

Emily cocked her head. "So she *is* your girlfriend.

I told Stella she was wrong."

"Who's Stella?" said Josh.

"A friend of mine from dance class," Emily told him. "She said she's seen you with the same girl a bunch of times. On the train."

"Well, you can tell Stella she is wrong," Josh said.

"Oh, I'll do that," said Emily. She turned to leave the room. At the door she turned around. "I just hope Mom and Dad don't find out about her," she said. "Stella said she didn't look like a homeless person to *her*."

Emily started to leave, but Josh called her back. She turned to him, an innocent look on her face. "Yes?" she said. "Is there something I can do for you?"

"Get your homework," Josh told her.

Emily beamed and ran out. She returned a few moments later carrying her NoteTaker. Josh moved over on the bed, and she sat next to him.

"What are you having a hard time with?" Josh asked her.

"Math," said Emily.

"Ah," Josh said. "That's why you don't want to ask Mom or Dad." He looked at the problem on her NoteTaker and started to tell her how to solve it. Then he paused. "Wait a minute," he said. "Since when have you had trouble with math?"

"Since now," Emily said.

Josh handed her back the NoteTaker. "I'm not buying it."

Emily groaned. "All right, I don't need help with my homework." She kicked her feet against the bed.

"Come on," Josh urged. "What's going on?"

"Fine," Emily said, as if he'd forced her to talk. "It's you. You've been acting all weird."

Josh felt a knot of fear form in his gut. What had Emily noticed? He'd been careful not to take Z too often at home. He'd done it a couple of times, but only when he was in his room alone. Then he'd sat up all night playing the hologame.

"Yeah, well," Josh said. "I am pretty weird."

"This is weirder than normal," said Emily. "I don't really know how to explain it. And now there's this girl."

"I told you, she's just a friend," Josh reminded her.

"And you don't talk to Firecracker anymore," Emily continued.

"Sure I do," said Josh. "Just because he hasn't been over for a few—"

"Come on, Josh. Poppy told me," Emily interrupted him.

Poppy. Firecracker's little sister. *Between her and this Stella girl, they're practically a detective agency,* Josh thought. He'd been worried about Firecracker when really he should have been concerned about a bunch of nine-year-olds.

"Firecracker and I kind of had a fight," he told Emily.

"About that girl?"

"No," Josh said. "It's nothing."

"Is that how you got that bruise on your face?"

Josh put his hand to his cheek. "Nah, I walked into an open locker door."

"Poppy said he's been really sad," Emily told him, looking at his bruise doubtfully.

"Sad?" Josh echoed. "Firecracker?"

"That's what she said," Emily confirmed.

"Well, don't worry about it," Josh told her.

"You shouldn't fight with your best friend," said Emily. "They're kind of hard to find."

"When did you turn into a fortune cookie?" Josh asked her.

"When did you get a girlfriend?" Emily countered.

"For the last time, she's not my girlfriend," said Josh.

"Stella said you kissed her," Emily pressed.

He was busted. But how? He and Charlie were always careful *not* to do anything like that where people might see them who shouldn't. "She never saw that," Josh said. "Because it never happened."

"Stella said she saw you," Emily said stubbornly.

"Did she get a picture of it?" asked Josh.

He saw the expression on Emily's face falter. He'd caught her. Stella might have seen him with Charlie, but she'd never seen them kiss.

"She's still your girlfriend," Emily said. "I know she is."

"You just keep thinking that," said Josh. "But don't go telling anyone things you can't prove."

"Maybe," his sister said, clearly annoyed that she'd been beaten.

"Hey," he said. "You want to watch a holofilm after dinner? I'll even let you pick."

Emily's face lit up. "Yes!" she said. "And I know just what I want to see."

"Nothing with princesses or dancing," Josh warned her.

Emily made a disgusted face. "What do I look like, an eight-year-old?" she said. "I want to see that documentary about the sharks they found in the Hell Sea on Mars."

Josh groaned. "Haven't you seen that, like, twelve times?" he asked.

"Thirteen," Emily corrected. "But I can watch it over and over. Those sharks are amazing. I mean, come on, they practically have lava for blood. What's not to love?"

"All right," said Josh. "We can watch your stupid sharks. Now get out of here. I have some stuff to do."

When Emily was gone, Josh lay back down and closed his eyes. Why had he and Charlie been so careless? Maybe it was time for them to just tell people they were together. Charlie said it was against Clatter's rules, but maybe he would make an exception.

Then again, the mood on the team had been a little strange. Stash still hadn't come back, and not only had Bess been injured in that afternoon's game, Freya had taken a bite when a meatbag hiding underwater in one of the sewers had jumped up and grabbed her from behind. So now they were down three team members. *Maybe it's not the best time to try to bend the rules,* Josh decided.

Then there was the Firecracker situation. It had been really hard for Josh to ignore his best friend, especially since they had a couple of classes together. But after Firecracker had tried to talk to him a few times and Josh had made it clear he wasn't going to talk, they had each started pretending that the other didn't exist. In class they sat as far apart as possible, and Josh had started eating lunch in an unused classroom in the school's lower level. Sometimes he had to share it with one or two of the stoners who liked to spend the lunch hour high on virtual-reality drugs, but they were mostly okay.

He knew that he was partly to blame for what had happened between him and Firecracker. It was only natural that Firecracker was curious. But now it was too late to apologize.

Or is it? he asked himself. Why couldn't he tell Firecracker he was sorry? He didn't have to tell him everything. He could just tell him about Charlie, and say that he was afraid *she* would get in trouble if anyone knew about them. That was sort of a good explanation for Josh's behavior that day.

He got up, went to his desk, and punched Firecracker's number into the com terminal. After three notifications the screen lit up and Josh found himself looking at the face of Firecracker's uncle, who he and Poppy lived with. He was a timid, nervous man, but when he saw Josh he smiled.

"Josh!" he said, sounding relieved.

"Hi, Mr. Reilly," said Josh. "Is Firecracker there?"

A worried look crossed the man's face. "No," he answered. "Isn't he there with you?"

"No," Josh said.

"He said he was staying over at your house tonight to work on a project for school," Mr. Reilly said.

Josh didn't know what to say. Why would Firecracker tell his uncle he was staying over at Josh's house? More important, where had he *really* gone? It wasn't like him to lie to his uncle. But Josh didn't want to upset Mr. Reilly, so he said, "I remember now. He was going to stop by our friend Mac's house and try out a new game. Then he's coming here. Duh. I totally forgot."

Mr. Reilly sighed, visibly relieved. "That's what I thought," he said.

"I'm sorry I bothered you," Josh said. "Have a good night, Mr. Reilly."

"You too, Josh. Tell Peter to call me when he gets in."

"Sure thing," said Josh, and cut off the comlink. He leaned back in his desk chair.

Things weren't adding up. Firecracker wouldn't just disappear. But now that he thought about it, he hadn't seen him at school that day either. He'd assumed Firecracker was sick or had a dentist's appointment or something. Now he worried that something bad might have happened to him.

A terrible thought came to him . . . but it was the only possible answer.

"Charlie told Scrawl about Firecracker following me," Josh whispered as a cold, hard knot gripped his insides.

16

"It's Josh."

"Hey," Charlie said. "I was going to send you a video message later."

"Did you tell anyone about Firecracker following me?" Josh asked her.

A flicker of fear crossed Charlie's face. She recovered quickly, but Josh had seen it. "You did, didn't you?"

"What makes you think that?" said Charlie. She cleared her throat.

"Firecracker is missing," Josh said. "And I think Scrawl has something to do with it."

"Scrawl?" said Charlie. "What would Scrawl have to do with Firecracker?"

"I was hoping you could tell me," Josh answered.

He watched Charlie's face on the com screen, waiting for her reply. She looked down. For a long time she didn't say anything. When she looked up again her eyes were clouded with fear. "I need to talk to you," she said. "Not on com. In person."

"Why can't we talk here?" Josh asked.

"We just can't," said Charlie. "Please, Josh. Just meet me. I might know something about Firecracker."

Josh hesitated. If Charlie knew something about his friend's disappearance, why couldn't she just tell him?

"Where?" he asked Charlie.

"Do you know where the Church of the Sorrowful Mother is?" Charlie answered.

"Yes," said Josh.

"Meet me there in half an hour," Charlie told him.

Josh hesitated for a moment. Should he trust Charlie? He wanted to. He *needed* to. But now he didn't know. If she had told Scrawl about Firecracker, then how could he believe anything she told him?

He looked at the clock. It was seven-thirty. If he hurried, he could get to Three Sisters Square and back before ten. He had no choice. He grabbed his jacket and knit hat and left his room. Nobody was in the living room, so he didn't bother telling anyone he was going out. He would be back before they noticed anyway.

It was raining again, and he wished he'd

remembered to bring an umbrella. He pulled his hat down, but still he got wet. He didn't care, though. He just wanted to get to the church and talk to Charlie. Hopefully she would know where Firecracker was.

He decided to take the hoverbus. Because of the rain, most people were heading underground. Only a few chose to stand at the curb getting wet. But Josh saw the blinking blue lights of a city hoverbus only a block away, so he joined the small group at the stop. He watched the bus approach, the jets on its underside emitting streams of warm air that kept it floating several feet above the street. In the cold the air turned to steam, giving the bus the appearance of an angry dragon. When it came to a stop, Josh got on and took a seat near the back door.

The ride took twenty minutes. It was raining even harder when Josh got off at Three Sisters Square, but the Church of the Sorrowful Mother wasn't far. Josh ran across the square, which was filled with penitents standing in the rain mumbling the strange chants of their religion. Their eyes were closed, and they took no notice of him as he ran up the stairs and passed through the huge stone archway above which the Mother stood, her hands covering her eyes.

Inside, the church smelled of incense and old wax. Oil lamps, centuries old, hung on long chains from the vaulted ceiling, their flames sending up plumes of black smoke. All along the stone sides of the sanctuary, stained-glass windows depicted strange scenes from the life of the Mother. Josh had studied some of them in his religious history class at school, but he had long since forgotten what they were.

Several anchorites were gathered around the circular stone altar at the front of the church. The altar was strewn with pink, red, and white roses, and the women were chanting in low voices. Josh wondered what the anchorites were saying. Supposedly they spoke a language only they understood.

He looked around for Charlie and spotted her kneeling before a low wall covered in white candles. As Josh watched, she lit one of the candles, held it in her hand as she said something, then placed it on the wall beside the others. Then she stood up and turned around. When she saw Josh, she smiled and walked toward him.

"It's for my mother," she said. "The candle. I light one for her every week."

"Oh," said Josh. He wasn't sure how he was supposed to respond.

"She was Gaian," Charlie explained. "I mean, she *is* Gaian." She smiled sadly.

"What does the candle do?"

Charlie laughed. "I don't know. Sends out light and happiness or something."

Josh nodded. Now that he was face-to-face with Charlie, he almost forgot why he was there. She was so pretty, with her wet hair shining in the candlelight. *You're here for Firecracker,* he reminded himself. *And she knows something about him.*

"So what about Firecracker?" he said.

"Not here," said Charlie, looking around. "Come with me."

She walked along the side of the sanctuary. Josh hesitated a moment. Charlie looked back and nodded for him to follow.

They passed the chanting anchorites and entered a low-ceilinged hallway built out of the same stone as the rest of the church. The hallway curved around the back of the sanctuary. Every twenty feet or so was a heavy wooden door with a small window about five feet up. Josh noticed that some of the windows were covered by solid metal plates. Charlie stopped before one of the doors with an open window, looked inside, and pushed the door open. She entered while Josh stood in the doorway, looking at the room beyond. It was small, no more than eight feet long by five feet wide, and it was completely bare.

"What is this?" he asked Charlie.

"A prayer room," Charlie said. "Come in."

Josh stepped into the room, and Charlie shut the door. She slid a heavy iron deadbolt into place and then slid the metal covering on the door's window closed.

"People come in here to pray or meditate," Charlie explained. "The anchorites sleep in these rooms at night. Well, some of them do, anyway."

"It's like being in a tomb," said Josh. He ran his hands over the stone walls. They were cold and damp. He couldn't see how anyone could sleep in such a place.

"You asked me if I told Scrawl about Firecracker," Charlie began. Josh looked at her. She wasn't looking away from him now. "I did," she said.

Josh shook his head. "Why would you—"

"He followed me," said Charlie.

Josh stood there, not sure he'd heard her correctly. "Followed you?" he said. "When?"

"A few days ago," Charlie said. "I was walking home, and he just appeared out of nowhere. He said he'd seen you talking to me on the train."

Stella said she saw us on the train, Josh thought.

"He wanted to know who I was," Charlie continued. "He wanted to know what you and I were doing together." She was talking more quickly now. "He accused me of . . . of . . . being some kind of bad influence on you."

"What did you tell him?" Josh asked.

Charlie shook her head. "He was yelling," she said. "I didn't know what to say." She looked at Josh. "So I ran."

"Why didn't you tell me?"

"I don't know," Charlie said.

Josh sighed. "But you told Scrawl."

"Yes. I just wanted him to know that someone might be trying to track us," said Charlie. "We're supposed to tell him when—"

"What did he do?" Josh said, interrupting her. "What did Scrawl do?"

"I think he just wanted to scare him," said Charlie.

"Scare him?" Josh said. "What, into not following you? Into forgetting that he saw us together? That doesn't make any sense, Charlie."

She turned away from him, saying nothing. Josh stared at her back, waiting for an answer. When she finally turned around, she was crying. "You don't understand," she said, wiping her nose with her hand. "But it's not your fault. I should have told you."

"Told me what?" Josh asked.

Charlie bit her lip. "It's not just the game that

Clatter doesn't want anyone to know about," she said. "There's something else."

"What something else?" said Josh.

Charlie crouched down and put her head in her hands. "You're going to hate me," she said quietly.

Josh crouched beside her. "I won't hate you," he told her. "But you have to tell me."

Charlie looked at him through tear-stained eyes. "It's the Z," she said, her voice hoarse. "He doesn't want anyone to know about the Z."

It took Josh a moment to put the pieces together. "You get the Z from Clatter," he said. "That's it, isn't it?"

"We all do," said Charlie. "Everyone who plays. He makes it and gives it to us."

"And he doesn't want anyone to find out that he makes it," Josh said.

"Right," Charlie said. "He gives it to us and also sells it to his customers who bet on the game. He's going to start selling it on the streets, too, and he'll make a lot of money. But if anyone finds out, he'll probably go to jail, and the game will be shut down."

Josh stood up. "Why didn't you tell me?" he asked.

Charlie stood up and pushed her hair back. "Before I tell you, you have to know something."

Josh didn't respond. "Everything I feel about you is real," she said. "Everything about *us* is real. I've never lied about that." She laughed. "Believe me, it would be easier for both of us if I were lying. But I really like you, Josh." She paused for a long moment. "You believe me, don't you?"

Josh looked at her worried eyes and her shaking hands. He did believe her. "I do," he said.

"Like I said, Clatter gives Z to everyone on the team," she said. "The only one who doesn't take it is Scrawl. He says it makes him feel sick. Anyway, Clatter doesn't make us pay for it, but . . ."

"But?" Josh encouraged her.

"But after a while he calls in a favor," Charlie said.

Josh didn't understand. "What kind of favor?"

"He makes us find a new person for the team," said Charlie. "If we don't, he cuts us off. And believe me, it isn't pretty when that happens. Bess refused to do it, and you saw what happened to her."

"Bess?" said Josh. "What are you talking about? He saved Bess."

Charlie shook her head. "No, he didn't," she said. "He killed her because she wouldn't recruit for him. He sent her into the tunnels knowing she wouldn't let the rest of us die. He didn't get to her in time, Josh. He never even tried. He let her drown."

"No," Josh said. "You're lying. He wouldn't do that.

He wouldn't let one of us *die*."

"He's done it before," Charlie said. "You don't know what he's really like, Josh. You have no idea."

Josh felt the air leave his lungs. Was Charlie telling the truth? Was Bess really dead? And was Clatter responsible? He couldn't believe it.

Then something else she'd said clicked into place. "You're telling me you recruited me as payment to Clatter for the Z?" he asked.

Charlie nodded slowly. "Yes," she said. "That's what I'm telling you."

17

Josh ran through the rain, not caring where he went. He just wanted to get away from Charlie. She followed him for two blocks, calling for him to stop, but he lost her by getting on a hoverbus and then, just as the doors were closing, pushing his way off through the back door. The last he'd seen of Charlie, she had her face pressed against the bus window, yelling his name.

His heart was pounding, and he felt like he might throw up. Charlie had used him to pay Clatter for her Z. If what she said was true, soon enough Clatter would demand that he do the same thing. And all this time Charlie had been telling him not to mention Z to anyone on the team. *She really played me,* he thought.

He looked around, trying to get his bearings. He had run eastward away from Three Sisters Square and was now a block away from Midcity Park. He could walk through it, exit through the south end, and be only a couple of blocks from his house. But how could he go home when his best friend was missing? His whole life had been sent into a tailspin.

The rain had chased most people out of the park, and the ones who remained were mainly Dusters (who never seemed to notice the weather), Boarders using the empty paths as raceways, and the occasional person walking a dog.

He stuffed his hands into his pockets, and his fingers landed on something small and hard. He pulled out the tablet of Z and looked at it. He started to throw it onto the ground, but found he couldn't do it. Despite the hatred he had for Z at that moment, the memory of how it helped him be a better player—and how it made him feel good even when he wasn't playing—made it impossible for him to just let go.

Instead, he took it.

As he kept walking, his mind slipped into a comforting fog. The part of Josh that worried about everything disappeared and was replaced by a feeling of invincibility. Nobody could hurt him. They would be *afraid* of him. The world around him became all about sensations. The rain on his skin. The smell of the air. The sounds of cars honking and voices chattering like birds. All of it swirled around in his head like a storm.

A Boarder whizzed past him, the wheels of his board *clack-clack-clack*ing on the pavement. They tossed up water behind them, and the spray caught the light from the streetlamps and dazzled Josh's eyes. The Boarder laughed, the sound rolling through Josh's head like waves. He laughed too. Everything was okay now. Charlie didn't matter. Scrawl didn't matter. Firecracker didn't matter.

Nothing mattered.

The peaceful feeling lasted until he reached the center of the park, where a group of Zooeys was dancing in the rain beneath a streetlamp. The frantic, pounding beat of techno music filled the air as the rabbits, cats, and kangaroos bounced up and down, their paws waving wildly and their heads going back and forth. Watching them, Josh began to feel afraid. The music seemed to wrap around his heart, replacing its steady pumping with jerky, painful lurches.

Anger bloomed in his mind, expanding like a flower opening to the sun. The Zooeys had ruined his moment of happiness. Their thumping music and frenzied dancing pulled at him, trying to drag him into the dizzying chaos. Josh fought it off, resisting. He had to make it stop.

With a roar he charged into the group, pushing

bodies to the ground and trying to find the source of the tormenting music. Frightened Zooeys screamed and crawled away from him as he yelled at them to shut up. He grabbed a lion by the throat and pulled him close, so that their faces were almost touching. He could feel the lion's heart beating like a drum in his mind, and smelled the stench of fear. "Where is it?" Josh shouted. "Where is it?"

The Zooey shook his head. "I don't know, man. I don't know!"

Josh shoved the lion away. Now the Zooeys were in a circle around him, staring in terror. He whirled around and around, daring them to come closer. "I'll kill you!" he screamed. "I'll kill all of you!"

And he really did want to hurt them. He ran for them and they scattered, fleeing into the dark. Watching them go, Josh began to laugh. *They're afraid of me,* he thought with delight. *They're afraid of me.* It made him feel strong. No one—nothing— could harm him.

"Hey!" a voice called out.

He turned to see three Boarders behind him. One, a boy wearing a T-shirt that said BOARD > BORED on it, shook his head. "That wasn't cool, man. They were just having fun."

Josh growled. The boy stepped back but didn't run.

"You should leave," said another Boarder, a girl with dreadlocks threaded through with beads in every color.

Josh laughed at her. She was weak. And she was telling *him* what to do.

"Maybe we should show him the way out," the third Boarder said. Not much bigger than Emily, he was stick thin.

Josh sneered at him. "Maybe you should try," he said.

He dashed in their direction. Unlike the Zooeys, though, they didn't run. They met his attack, closing in as he aimed for the smallest one. As his head butted into the boy's chest, the others tackled him. Josh fell to the pavement. His face hit the ground hard, and he felt his cheek scraped raw.

Rolling onto his back, Josh kicked and clawed at the Boarders. His fingers found the girl's hair and pulled hard. She yelped in pain, then slammed her fist into his nose. Blood spurted out. Josh could taste it on his lips, thick and metallic. The smell, too, was overwhelming, making him hungry and sick at the same time.

The first Boarder was on top of Josh now, trying to pin his arms to the ground. Josh bucked, throwing him off, and rolled on top of him. He put his hands around the boy's throat and started to squeeze. He saw the boy's eyes widen in fear as his air was cut off.

Josh wanted to see him die. By choking him, he could destroy everything that was gnawing at him. His mind skipped from thought to thought, and image to image. Charlie. The burst of fire from a flamethrower. Firecracker. The melting face of a z. It was like watching a holofilm gone crazy. Only by killing the Boarder could he make it stop.

Then he was flung sideways as a shower of falling stars crossed his vision. There was a loud roaring in his ears, as if a huge unseen wave had crashed over him. He looked up and saw the skinny Boarder staring down at him. The boy was holding the end of his board in both hands and raising it up for a second blow. Josh watched as it came toward him.

Josh woke up choking. His mouth was filled with water, and he couldn't breathe through his nose. He spat, trying to clear his throat, and gagged. A horrible iron taste coated his mouth. He wiped his lips with his hand and it came away red. *That's blood,* he thought, wondering whose it was.

The rain was falling hard, and it was dark. He tried to sit up, but pain rocketed through his head. He touched his nose, and again his fingers were painted red. The rain washed away the blood, turning it pink as it dripped onto Josh's shirt. His head swam, and he thought he might pass out, so he sat quietly, just trying to breathe.

He was also cold. The rain had soaked him, and he was shivering. He rubbed his hands on his arms to warm them, but it did no good. His teeth were chattering, clicking together in an erratic dance. He blew his nose to clear it, and a thick glob of half-clotted blood splattered onto his jeans. He tried to wipe it away, but it only smeared.

He looked around at the empty park. How long had he been lying there? Had anyone come along and seen him? Why hadn't they helped? *I could have died,* he thought. *Why didn't anyone do something?*

He wondered what time it was and looked at his watch. The glass was smashed, and he could just make out the numbers. It was ten.

He forced himself to stand up. Again he saw bursts of light in his head, and he almost sat down again. But he had to get out of there. He had to get home. There was something he needed to do, although he couldn't remember what it was.

Then it came to him. What Charlie had said. About how she'd set him up to settle her debt with Clatter.

As if he were just hearing the news for the first time, Josh felt overcome by shock and anger. Charlie had lied to him, and she might have gotten Firecracker in trouble as well. Josh had to find out. He had to help his friend.

He walked slowly, trying not to jar his body too much. After a few minutes he felt a little better, although he could tell that his face was pretty badly cut up. How was he going to explain *that* to his parents?

Tell them you were knocked down, he thought.

The story would probably keep him from getting in too much trouble tonight. Then he'd just have to figure out what to do about Charlie and how to find out what happened to Firecracker.

Something else occurred to him. Once Clatter found out that Josh knew about the Z, and about what Scrawl might or might not have done to Firecracker, it was pretty much guaranteed that Josh would be next on his list of problems to solve. Which meant one thing—Josh had to get to Clatter before Clatter got to him.

18

Josh didn't go home.

He made it as far as his block, even as far as the sidewalk in front of his house, but as he set his foot on the first step, he realized with absolute certainty that if he didn't do something *now*, it might be too late. Firecracker was still missing, and Charlie had told him too much. Maybe she would just keep their conversation to herself, but maybe she would run to Clatter and tell him everything.

He turned his back on his house and walked to the corner. How was he going to find Scrawl? He didn't even know where he lived. And what if Charlie had already gotten to him? Then he would know what Josh was after.

Still, he had to try. He leaned against a light post and thought. His head was throbbing, but he forced himself to concentrate. What did he know about Scrawl?

Nothing, he thought with some surprise. *He's a blank page.* If someone had asked him a minute before what his relationship with Scrawl was, Josh would have said they were friends. But now he realized that although Scrawl was always nice to him, Josh knew very little about him. It was as if Scrawl had deliberately kept himself a mystery.

But there had to be something, some clue Scrawl had let drop, maybe in conversation. Josh tried to remember anything they'd talked about. His mind came up empty, and he felt frustration growing in him. It was stupid to think he could handle this on his own. He should just call the police and tell them what he knew.

Then, from the depths of his memories, something rose up. Something Scrawl had said to him when they met. What had they been talking about? *Comics,* he thought.

That was it—the Pageteria. Scrawl had said that he lived a couple of blocks away from it. It was in Farside, on the other side of the city. That seemed like a good place to start.

He went to the subway station and looked at the interactive map. Punching in where he wanted to go, he waited for the route to be highlighted on the map. After memorizing it, he passed through the gates, scanned his fare card, and went to the right platform. Fortunately, the train came only a minute later.

The car was sparsely populated, and by the time the train reached the first stop in Farside, it was almost empty. Josh waited until the cyberconductor called out the stop he wanted, then exited into a dingy station. Water dripped from the ceiling, and the lights flickered in protest. The white tiles of the walls were dirty and broken, and the place smelled like garbage. Josh hurried up the stairs to the street.

He walked the four blocks to the Pageteria. It was closed, but he hadn't come there to check out the collections. He just wanted to use it as a reference point for looking for Scrawl's house. But now that he was there, he didn't have a clue where to begin.

Just ask, he told himself. *Someone around here must know him.*

"Right," he said aloud. "Because there are only, like, four hundred houses around here. Why don't I just knock on all the doors, one at a time?"

He looked around. The streets were mostly empty, although a block away he saw a small group of people hanging around outside what looked like a bar. As he got nearer, he saw that it was three women talking to a man. The man had a mechabird on his shoulder—a beautiful blue and gold parrot—and the women were talking to it.

"Who's a pretty bird?" one woman said.

The parrot cocked its head. "You are," it squawked. The women laughed as the man grinned. Then the man noticed Josh standing there. "What are you looking at?" he said gruffly as the women eyed Josh up and down.

"Nothing," Josh said. "Actually, I'm looking for someone."

The man laughed. "Who isn't, kid? Aren't you out a little late for a school night? Why don't you just run on home now."

Josh forced himself to keep talking. "His name is Scrawl," he said. "I was supposed to meet him here, and—"

"Never heard of him," the man interrupted him. The parrot ruffled its feathers. "Never heard of him," it echoed.

Josh turned around. "Thanks," he muttered as he walked off, trying to think where to go next.

"Wait a minute," a voice called out.

Josh turned to see one of the women walking toward him. She was balanced on heels so high, Josh wondered how she kept from tipping over, but she wobbled only slightly as she approached. "You want to talk to Scrawl?" she asked.

Josh nodded. "You know him?"

The woman smiled. "Everybody around here knows Scrawl," she said. "But only about half of them will admit it. Let me guess—you want to talk to him about getting something."

"Umm, sort of," said Josh.

"You and half the city," the woman said. She regarded him for a long moment. "You look like a nice kid," she said. "And you look like you've had a hard night. You go on over to 1372 Barber Street. It's two blocks that way. Apartment 3D. Tell him Lola said it was okay."

She smiled at Josh, who smiled back. "Thanks," he said. "Thanks a lot."

"No problem," Lola said.

Josh watched her walk back to her friends, then walked to Barber Street. A few minutes later he was standing in front of apartment 3D. Taking a deep breath, he rang the doorbell. A moment later the door opened and he was looking at Scrawl.

"How'd you get here?" Scrawl said, clearly surprised to see him.

"Lola," Josh said. He wasn't in the mood for giving explanations; he wanted to hear some. "I want to talk to you about Firecracker. And Z."

If Scrawl was shocked, he didn't show it. He simply

nodded and held the door open. "Come inside," he said.

Josh entered the apartment. The furniture was stylish, and the walls were covered in framed artwork. Josh looked at the closest piece and saw that it was a drawing in ink of a costumed figure.

"Green Lantern," Scrawl said. "It's just a sketch, but it cost me four months' pay. It's an original Gil Kane." He handed Josh a towel. "Dry off," he said.

Josh toweled off his head, wincing a little at the pain.

"What happened to you?" Scrawl asked.

"Just a little accident," said Josh.

"I assume you didn't stop by just to say hi," Scrawl said.

Josh looked him in the eye. "What did you do to Firecracker?"

Scrawl didn't blink. "We had a little chat," he said.

"What about?" Josh said.

Scrawl shrugged. "I just asked him to stop following Charlie around."

"Huh," Josh replied. "I thought maybe you talked about Z and how Clatter is planning on selling it on the streets."

This time Scrawl did blink. But he quickly regained his composure. "That didn't come up," he said. "But it sounds like somebody's been talking to *you* about it."

"Where's Firecracker now?" Josh asked.

"How would I know?" said Scrawl.

"Don't lie," Josh snapped. "He never went home."

Scrawl had a puzzled look on his face. "He's missing?"

Josh nodded. "Yeah, he's missing. And I think you know why."

Scrawl sat down on a chair. "No," he said, although he seemed to be talking to himself and not to Josh. "He said he wasn't going to take him."

"Who said that?" Josh demanded. "Take him where?"

Scrawl looked up. "Charlie told you about the Z, didn't she?"

Josh hesitated. If he admitted it, then Scrawl might do something to Charlie. But she was the only likely source of the information, and they both knew it. "Yes," he said.

Scrawl stood up. "We have to find her," he said.

"Wait a minute," Josh protested. "What about Firecracker? And why do we have to find Charlie? She was fine when I saw her."

"When was that?" asked Scrawl.

"About two hours ago," said Josh.

Scrawl shook his head. "They could already have her."

Josh held his hands up. "What the hell are you talking about?" he said. "If you're trying to get me to forget about Firecracker—"

"I didn't do anything to your friend!" Scrawl shouted. It was the first time Josh had ever heard him lose control. All he could do was stand there, looking at Scrawl's normally cool face twisted in anger.

"Listen to me," Scrawl said in a softer tone. "There's more going on here than you know. Way more. It's not just about Z or the game. But it's gone too far now, and I can't let him hurt anyone else."

"Clatter?" Josh asked.

Scrawl nodded.

"Charlie said he killed Bess," said Josh. "Is that true?"

Scrawl looked away. "We didn't take her to the hospital," he said quietly. "We put her in the incinerator."

"And you just let him?" Josh said angrily. "You didn't try to stop him?"

"You have a little sister, right?" Scrawl asked in reply.

Josh nodded. "So what?"

"Well, so do I," said Scrawl. "Two of them. Jilly and Annie. They're nine and eleven. Do you want to know what Clatter said he would do to them if I told anybody about him, about what he does?"

Josh shook his head. "I think I can imagine," he said.

"I thought I could go along with his game," Scrawl said. "Believe it or not, he's been good to me. I owe him a lot. But I've paid him back enough. And now we're going to stop him." He took a deep breath. "But first I have to show you something you really don't want to see."

19

Josh looked down into the hole. A foul smell wafted up through it. "I'm not going down there," he told Scrawl. Scrawl was kneeling in the street, holding the manhole cover he'd removed a moment ago. "Just do it," he ordered Josh. He looked over his shoulder. "That light is going to change in about fifteen seconds, and I don't really feel like getting flattened. Now *go!*"

Josh hesitated just a moment longer, then stepped onto the first rung of the ladder. When he was halfway down, Scrawl followed him, pulling the manhole cover back over the opening. Seconds later Josh heard the sound of wheels over their heads. He reached the bottom of the ladder and stepped into a puddle of water that covered his shoes and the bottoms of his jeans.

"Nice place for a front door," he remarked as Scrawl joined him.

"That's the point," Scrawl said. "It's the *back* door.

And where better to put it than in the middle of one of the busiest streets in the city?"

Josh had to admit it was a clever idea. When Scrawl had told him they were going to go into the sewers through a hole in Broad Avenue, he was sure he'd heard wrong. But as soon as the light turned red to allow the cross traffic from Seventh Street to go, Scrawl had run out, heaved the manhole cover up, and told Josh to get in.

Josh still wasn't sure he should trust Scrawl. But following him seemed to be his only option.

"Did it have to be a sewer?" Josh asked.

"Actually, it's a storm drain," Scrawl corrected him.

Scrawl had brought two flashlights along. They each had one, and Josh used his to scan the tunnel ahead of them for anything he didn't want to step in. Several times the beam of light shone on rats, which looked at Josh and Scrawl with wary eyes and scurried out of sight beneath the piles of trash that littered the floor.

"Where are we going?" Josh asked Scrawl for the tenth time since leaving the apartment.

"I told you, you don't want to know," said Scrawl.

"I have to find out sometime," Josh objected.

Scrawl stopped. He turned and looked at Josh, his

flashlight casting a ghostly shadow on his face. "Okay," he said. "You're right. I'm taking you to Clatter's factory."

"His factory?"

"Where he makes Z," said Scrawl.

"That's insane," Josh said. "We should be getting help."

Scrawl hesitated. "I think Firecracker is there," he said. "Maybe Charlie too."

Josh felt his heart skip a beat. "Why would he have them there?"

"That's the part you don't want to know about," said Scrawl. "You'll just have to see for yourself."

He resumed the trek through the sewer. Soon the floor began to slope down, and Josh had to work hard to keep his balance. They descended at a steep angle before the tunnel leveled out again and continued on. Then they walked for another fifteen minutes, making several turns, until they came to a steel door marked with a sign that read CES CREWS ONLY.

"City Electrical System?" Josh said. "What is this, a power hub or something?"

"Or something," said Scrawl. He was typing something into a keypad to the side of the door. A moment later it opened with a hiss. Scrawl stepped inside and motioned for Josh to follow.

They were in a small room. On the side opposite the first door was another door, exactly the same. The first door shut behind Josh as Scrawl went to the second. "This is an airlock," Scrawl explained. The two doors can't be open at the same time, and each one has a different code." He looked up at the ceiling, where a several small nozzles protruded from the smooth metal surface. "If you enter the wrong code, those emit gas," he said. "It will knock you out cold in under ten seconds."

"That would certainly keep people out," Josh said. "So why do you know the codes?"

Scrawl finished typing. "Let's just say Clatter trusts me," he said. "Well, as much as he trusts anyone."

The room Josh entered next was huge. It was also as modern looking as the sewer entrance was dilapidated. The walls were covered in polished metal, and the lighting was low and soothing. Several fans were running, and the air smelled clean and fresh.

"It's like a hospital," Josh said.

Scrawl snorted. "You're not far off," he said.

Josh could see a row of five metal operating tables on the far side of the room. As they drew closer, he saw that a body lay on one of the tables. It was a zombie. Its wrists and ankles were constrained by metal cuffs attached to the table, and another metal cuff was around its neck, holding it down.

The zombie was a teenage girl. Her long blond hair was matted, some of it clotted with dried blood from a wound on her scalp. Her skinny body was dressed in dirty jeans and a pink Hello Kitty T-shirt. Her skin was mottled with ugly bruises, and one eye was sewn shut with thick black thread. The other eye looked up at the ceiling, unmoving.

On each cuff was a small circular opening, and into each opening was inserted a long, thin needle attached to a length of clear tubing. Yellowish fluid filled the tubes, which ran beneath the table and disappeared into the floor.

"He makes the zombies here too?" Josh asked.

Scrawl nodded.

Josh reached out to touch the zombie's skin, but Scrawl grabbed his wrist. "Don't," he said.

"Relax," Josh said, irritated. "I just wanted to feel her skin. It's amazing how he makes them look so real." He pointed to the tubes. "What's that stuff, hydraulic fluid for the robotics?"

"It's blood," said Scrawl.

"Blood?" Josh repeated. "What are you talking about?"

"These are bleeding tables," Scrawl told him. "He's not pumping anything *in,* he's draining it *out.*"

Josh recoiled, staring at the girl. "I don't get it," he said. "I thought you said that this is where he makes Z."

"It is," said Scrawl. "But to make Z he needs blood. Zombie blood. And this is how he gets it."

Josh waited for Scrawl to say he was joking. When he didn't, Josh pointed to the girl and said, "You're telling me that's a *real* zombie?"

"She's real, all right," Scrawl answered.

Josh stared at him. Scrawl had to be kidding. But the look on his face was deadly serious. Could he be telling the truth?

Josh laughed nervously. "You're messing with me," he said. "Right?"

Scrawl shook his head.

"There haven't been any in years," Josh said.

"There are now." Said Scrawl.

Josh looked at the zombie on the table. He couldn't believe he had almost touched it. "Where do they come from?"

Scrawl looked at him. "This is the part you *really* don't want to see," he said. "Don't freak out on me, okay?"

"I'm already beyond freaked out," Josh told him. "It can't get any worse."

"Yeah, it can," Scrawl replied. He walked toward a

door to the right of the tables. When he reached it, he paused, took a deep breath, and pushed it open.

The stench was enough to make Josh gag. At first he was so busy coughing that he didn't have time to look for the source of the smell. When he could more or less breathe again, he looked up. They were in a room lined with cells, about twenty on each side. And inside each one was a zombie.

Josh felt like he'd been punched in the stomach. "They're real?" he said. "All of them? But that's impossible. All the z's were wiped out. The virus was wiped out."

Scrawl shook his head. "That's just what the government wants people to think," he said. "They never wiped out the virus, just the people who had it. Clatter's father worked on the project. He found a way to infect people and make them zombies."

Josh crept closer to the cell that Scrawl was looking into. Inside it was a man wearing a tattered suit. His skin bubbled with lesions, and his eyes were filmed over. He opened his mouth, revealing stumps of blackened teeth and a swollen purple tongue. Seeing Josh and Scrawl, he beat his hands against the glass, coating it with blood-flecked drool.

"He's alive?" Josh asked, still unable to believe it.

"Alive as he can be," said Scrawl.

"And Clatter made him like this?"

Scrawl nodded. "Yeah," he said.

Josh looked into the next cell. There a woman with a rat's nest of hair sat in the corner, pulling her own fingernails off. Half a dozen of them littered the floor. Josh felt his stomach rise.

"But why?" he sputtered. "Why would anyone want to *make* meatbags?"

"Money," Scrawl said. "Like I said, Clatter's dad studied the zombie virus. He was a chemist. He wanted to find a way to wipe it out. But the government wanted him to do just the opposite. They wanted him to make a weapon that would turn people *into* z's. Something they could put into the water or the air or food to infect a lot of people at once."

"Biological warfare," Josh said. "That's sick."

"That's what Clatter's father thought too," said Scrawl. "He refused to do it. So they decided to give him a little incentive to cooperate. They kidnapped Clatter. He was maybe five or six. They told Clatter's father that if he did what they wanted, they would give him his kid back."

"An offer he couldn't refuse," Josh said.

Scrawl nodded. "That's right," he said. "He just wanted to save his son. He did what they asked, but they killed him. They killed his wife too. They would have gotten Clatter, but he got away. I don't know who he was before, but since then he's been Clatter."

"And now he's making zombies using his dad's technology," Josh said. "That's messed up."

"I think what happened to him made him a little crazy," Scrawl replied. "He's super smart, there's no doubt about that. But he's also twisted. He says making money off of z's is payback for what the government did to him and his parents. The more zombies he makes, the more Z he makes."

"Z is zombie blood," Josh said, shuddering at the thought. Then he remembered that he had taken some himself, and panic filled him. "Z turns people into zombies?" he said.

"No," Scrawl answered. "Don't worry," he assured Josh. "We've all tried it. It won't turn you. Clatter has other ways of doing that. Z is made from z blood, but it's a diluted form of it. Just enough to make you feel a little bit of what they feel, but not enough to turn you."

Josh slumped to the ground with his back against the door of one of the cells. He heard the zombie inside start clawing at the metal. He tried not to listen. Scrawl came and sat beside him. "How long has he been doing this?" Josh asked him.

"A couple years," said Scrawl. "It took him a long time to figure out how to do it efficiently. The first versions of Z really did turn users into meatbags. Then Clatter got it to where it only made them crazy. Now he's got it pretty much figured out."

"Pretty much," Josh said. "Great. And how does the game come into this?"

"It's another way to make money," said Scrawl. "And it's a way to get rid of z's that are too far gone. That's when he puts them into the game."

Josh didn't want to accept what he was hearing. "We've been killing . . . people?" he said. "*I've* been killing people?"

Scrawl took him by the shoulders. "You wanted to know," he said as Josh took great gulps of air. "Now you do."

"And you knew about it," Josh said. "That makes you as bad as he is."

"He helped me, Josh," Scrawl said. "He's helped all of us."

"You mean he's bought you," said Josh, thinking about Scrawl's nice apartment. Then he remembered how excited he'd been seeing his first paycheck, and he felt a little ashamed. "How many of the others know?" he asked.

"Only Seamus and Finnegan," Scrawl answered. "I know they don't look like it, but they're science geeks. He's teaching them how to make the Z and how to replicate the virus. I help him with business stuff. The others he just uses for the game."

A thought occurred to Josh. "So if somebody gets bit in the game, they're being bit by a real zombie?"

Scrawl didn't say anything.

"What really happened to Stash and Freya?" Josh asked.

"Josh, it doesn't—"

"What happened to them!" Josh yelled. "Tell me!"

Scrawl nodded toward the cells at the end of the row. "Over there," he said.

Josh got up and walked slowly toward the cells. When he got there, he steadied himself and then looked through the window. Freya—or what had once *been* Freya—lunged at him, her teeth bared. She'd torn out her hair, which lay in bloody clumps on the floor, and her bald scalp was black with dried blood. Josh looked away.

He forced himself to look into the next cell. Stash was in it, standing motionless in the middle of the tiny space. The place on his shoulder where he'd been bitten was green and gangrenous, and his skin was mottled with dark purple lesions. One of his eyes was missing, the socket where it had been like raw hamburger.

"Who are the rest of them?" he asked Scrawl.

"Different people," he answered. "People who didn't pay their wagers. Street people. Runaway kids. People nobody will miss."

"So first he infects them, then he milks them for their blood," said Josh. "It's a slaughterhouse. Like they have for animals. Only these aren't animals, they're people."

"Yes, they're people. What did you think zombies were?" said Scrawl.

"I thought those were cybers!" Josh said. "And the ones in the hologame aren't real. It's just pretend."

"Still, I bet you never really thought about who they *used* to be," Scrawl said softly. "I know I didn't."

Josh started to argue, but stopped. Scrawl was right. He knew about his aunt Lucy, and yet he had never thought of her—not even once—when he was torching the z's in the game.

Freya pounded on the window of her cell and let out a strangled scream. Josh turned away. "Is this what happens to Torchers who 'retire' from the team?" he asked.

Scrawl didn't answer, but he didn't have to. Scrawl's silence confirmed it.

"So we help him make his money, we kill his victims when he's done with them, and if we try to get out, we end up like them." He jerked his head toward

Freya's and Stash's cells.

"We need to find your friend," Scrawl said. "And Charlie, if she's here. He hasn't turned them yet, or they'd be in here. That means he's probably holding them somewhere else while he decides what to do with them."

"Well, I *was* doing exactly that," said a voice. Clatter was standing in the doorway, peering at them through his gray glasses. He smiled and nodded at Scrawl, then Josh. "However, I think you gentlemen have just decided for me."

20

"**W**here are they?"

Josh faced Clatter. The anger in him was growing quickly, particularly because Clatter just stood there grinning. Josh wanted to wipe the smirk off his face. He even started toward the man, but Scrawl grabbed him and pulled him back. "Don't do it," he told Josh. "You won't win."

"You should listen to Arthur," Clatter said. Then he addressed Scrawl. "I assume this means you've decided to end our partnership."

Scrawl said nothing. After a moment Clatter sighed. "I *am* disappointed," he said. "You showed such promise. Now, well . . ." He waved his hand around the room full of cells. "It's unfortunate."

"You're not turning me into one of those things," said Scrawl. "I'd rather die."

"That could certainly be arranged," Clatter

replied. "But the alternative is so much more interesting. No, I'm afraid I can't make an exception for you, Arthur."

Scrawl stiffened but remained silent, staring at Clatter.

"What do you want?" Josh asked Clatter.

Clatter turned his attention to Josh. "Who says I want anything?" he asked. "Am I to understand that you think this is some kind of negotiation?" He laughed.

"I want Charlie and Firecracker," Josh said firmly, though terror threatened to take control of him. Now that he knew what Clatter was doing, the possibility that he might not leave the underground lab alive seemed very real.

"You *want*?" Clatter said. "I don't think you're in any position to be *wanting* anything."

"Well, maybe I have something *you* want," Josh countered.

Clatter raised an eyebrow. "And that would be?" he asked.

"Money," said Josh.

Clatter leaned against the doorway. "Are you offering me a bribe?"

Josh shook his head. "You know I don't have *that* kind of money," he said. "But I'm worth it."

"A ransom," said Clatter.

"No," Josh said. "Not a ransom. I mean my game playing. And his," he added, nodding toward Scrawl. "We're the best gamers you have."

Clatter shrugged. "You're good," he said.

"Really good," Josh said. "We bring in more money than anyone else on the team." He didn't know if this was entirely true, but he figured it was worth a shot. When Clatter didn't contradict him, he assumed he had guessed correctly.

"Let's play a game," he continued. "Me and Scrawl against your zombies. Call in your biggest wagerers. Make a big deal about it. A match to the death or whatever."

Clatter thought for a moment. Josh held his breath, hoping his idea would work. "Go on," Clatter said.

"If we win, you let us go," said Josh. "All of us. We won't say anything about what you're doing down here."

Clatter chuckled. "Or I could just kill you and not worry about that anyway," he said.

"Except that before we came here I sent my parents a com message telling them where we were going," said Josh. "It's set to open at five o'clock tomorrow morning."

Clatter shook his head. "You're lying," he said.

"No, he isn't," said Scrawl. "My sister will get the same message. It has maps and everything. The cops would be here by six, and there's no way you could clear everything out of here by then. Even if you killed us, your entire business would be wiped out. Plus, I think there are some people who would love to get their hands on you."

Clatter looked from one of them to the other. *He's trying to decide if we're bluffing,* Josh thought. He decided to beat Clatter to the punch. "No, you don't know whether we really did it or not," he said. "But you have more to lose by assuming we didn't than you do by assuming we did."

To his surprise, Clatter grinned. "That was very well put," he said. "All right. We'll play a game. But it won't be just you and Arthur playing. Your friends will join you. All four of you must survive, *and* all the zombies will have to be killed. If you can manage that, I will let you all go."

"How do we know you'll hold up your end of the bargain?" Josh asked.

"You don't," said Clatter. "But you have more to gain by assuming I will than you do by assuming I won't. So, do we have a deal?"

Josh looked at Scrawl, who nodded.

"Excellent," Clatter said. "At this hour it will take a

little while to gather together an audience. But I think that makes it even more exciting, don't you? I'll send the message out immediately. In the meantime, I imagine you'd like to see your friends. Come with me."

He walked to one of the cells and typed a code into the keypad beside it. Josh and Scrawl stepped back as the door opened.

"Don't worry," Clatter said as he stepped inside the cell. "It's unoccupied."

Josh and Scrawl followed him into the cell; then the door slid shut and the floor began to drop. It took a second for Josh to realize that they were in an elevator. It continued down for twenty or thirty seconds, then came to a halt. The doors opened and Clatter stepped out into a tunnel very much like the one through which Josh and Scrawl had entered the lab.

Josh was surprised that Clatter had turned his back on them. *Maybe we could jump him,* he thought.

"He has weapons," Scrawl whispered just loudly enough for Josh to hear him. Josh nodded to let him know he understood, even though part of him still wanted to knock Clatter down and hurt him.

"You know, Josh, I could use someone like you on my team," Clatter said. He turned and paused. "My *other* team, I mean. I plan to introduce Z to the streets shortly. You've tried it. You know how popular it will be. The profit potential is extraordinary. Are you sure you won't consider joining me?"

"I'll never be like you," said Josh.

"You wound me," Clatter said, feigning sadness. "And here I thought I was such a role model to all of you."

They walked for a few minutes and came to a stone archway covered by an old iron grate. Behind the grate was a small room cut into the rock, and Charlie and Firecracker were sitting on the floor, not looking at each other. When they heard noise in the tunnel, they glanced up. Josh saw expressions of hope flash across their faces but quickly disappear when they saw that Josh and Scrawl were with Clatter.

"I've brought you some company," Clatter said as he removed one of the keys tied to his coat and inserted it into the ancient lock. The lock opened reluctantly, and Clatter pulled the grate open just far enough for Josh and Scrawl to go inside. He shut it behind them and locked it. "I'll go make the arrangements," he said. "I suggest you fill your friends in on what we've agreed to."

As soon as Clatter disappeared, Charlie and Firecracker started talking at the same time.

"Where did you go, and what happened to your face?"

"Dude, what the hell are these people doing?"

"I didn't mean to—"

"I was only trying to—"

"Quiet!" Josh said. "Just listen. We don't have a lot of time."

He explained to Firecracker and Charlie about the zombies and Z, and about the deal he'd made with Clatter.

"What do you mean we have to fight our way out?" asked Firecracker. "Like for real?"

"For real," said Josh.

"This is insane," Charlie said.

"Look around," Scrawl told her. "This whole thing is insane."

Charlie shook her head. "This isn't happening," she said. "It's, I don't know, a dream. Or a bad Z trip. I just have to wake up." She started beating at herself with her hands.

Josh grabbed her and held her. She struggled for a moment, then slumped against him. He felt her shake as she sobbed.

"We can do this," he whispered. "We've done it a thousand times."

"Are you telling me you guys have been playing the game with real zombies?" Firecracker asked. "And real flamethrowers? And now we're playing to get out of here alive?"

"Yeah," Scrawl said. "That's pretty much it."

"That's awesome," Firecracker said.

"It's not awesome!" Charlie yelled. "Don't you get it? We have to kill people!"

Firecracker snorted. "We have to kill *meatbags*," he said. "Big deal."

"Some of those meatbags are our friends," said Scrawl.

"Come on, man," Firecracker said.

"What's wrong with you?" Charlie said. She pulled away from Josh and shoved Firecracker against the wall.

"Hey!" he said.

"This isn't a stupid game," Charlie continued. "It never was. We just thought it was. Those *meatbags* you're so hot to torch used to be like us." She looked at Josh and Scrawl. "Some of them *were* us. And that slimeball out there has made a lot of money from people like you who think it's a whole lot of fun."

Firecracker put his hands up in defeat. "Don't take it out on me," he said. "I wouldn't be here at all if you hadn't told Freakula there that I was stalking you." He looked at Josh. "Which I wasn't. I was just worried about you."

Josh nodded. "I know," he said. "It's okay. Right

now we have to talk about our plan."

"What field are we playing on?" Charlie asked.

Scrawl shook his head. "We don't know," he said. "But my guess is he'll put us on Location Eleven."

Charlie's head whipped up. "Eleven?" she said.

Josh looked from her to Scrawl. "What's eleven? I don't remember that from the manual."

"It's not in the manual," Scrawl said. "We've never played it before."

"Where is it?" Josh asked.

Scrawl rubbed his nose. "Feverfew," he said.

"The insane asylum?" said Firecracker. "That place on the cliffs? It's been condemned for at least thirty years. It's totally falling apart."

"Exactly," said Scrawl. "We haven't used it before because it's too dangerous for the Torchers. That's why Clatter wants to use it as a field."

"So the odds are against us," Charlie said.

"Then we just have to play the best game we've ever played," said Josh. He looked at each of them in turn. "We can do it. We just have to stick together."

21

Clatter came for them half an hour later. Seamus and Finnegan were with him. The two of them behaved oddly, not looking at the four captives and rocking back and forth slightly on their feet.

They're doped up on Z, Josh thought as Clatter unlocked the cell and told them to come out one by one. Josh went first. As he exited, Finnegan took his arm and placed a handcuff around his wrist. Josh tried to pull his hand back, but Finnegan gripped it tightly, then cuffed the other wrist also.

"Just a precaution," Clatter said. "Nothing to worry about."

"Five o'clock," Josh reminded Clatter. "That's when the message goes out and the cops come."

"Oh, I think this will be over long before then," Clatter said.

The three others joined Josh, all of them

handcuffed. Clatter ordered them to follow Seamus, who led them in the opposite direction from the elevator. A hundred yards on, the tunnel opened up into a larger tunnel running perpendicular to the first one. A short flight of stone steps led down to a small landing past which a stream of dirty water flowed along sluggishly. An old wooden rowboat was tied to the platform with a rope.

"Couldn't afford a hoverboat, huh?" Firecracker asked sarcastically.

Seamus pushed him roughly down the steps, with Finnegan urging the others along behind him. "We like it old school," Seamus said, nodding at the boat. "Get in and shut up."

Josh stepped in first. The boat rocked beneath him, and with his hands cuffed he couldn't keep his balance. He fell sideways, hitting one of the boat's bench seats with a painful thud. Seamus laughed, a dull chuckle that made Josh's skin crawl. He'd always found the twins a little strange, but now they were totally creeping him out.

Charlie got in next and sat beside Josh. Firecracker and Scrawl followed, squeezing in next to them, then Finnegan and Clatter, who took the seat at the front. Seamus untied the rope tethering the boat to the platform and got in last, taking the middle bench and facing Josh. As the boat floated out into the stream, he took the ends of the two oars attached to the sides of the boat by heavy steel oarlocks and began to row.

The tunnel was lit by a string of electric lights that ran along the ceiling. The ancient bulbs were mostly dead, but a few still worked. As the boat floated along, Josh occasionally caught a glimpse of what was around them.

"This tunnel was once used by the old underground rail system," Clatter announced from the front of the boat. "Like all the old tunnels, it flooded when Antarctica melted and the seas rose. But what was a tragedy for so many has been a boon for those of us who wish to conduct business unnoticed. The tunnels run nearly everywhere one might wish to go beneath the city."

Clatter continued to talk, but Josh tuned him out. He didn't care what Clatter had to say, but remained focused on what lay ahead. Without knowing the layout of where they would be playing, the team of Torchers couldn't form a real plan. But Scrawl had seen some basic maps of Feverfew, and assuming that that's where they were going, had used a piece of broken stone to sketch out a rough idea of what it might look like inside on the floor of the cell.

Seamus made several turns, moving into various

tunnels until Josh's sense of direction was completely lost. Sometimes they flowed with the water, and sometimes Seamus had to struggle against it. They passed half a dozen platforms similar to the one from which they'd launched the rowboat, and Josh wondered what part of the city each one led to.

Finally they traversed a very long tunnel where the water flowed more quickly. *It's going out to the ocean,* Josh thought. *This is where it empties out. We must be somewhere near the cliffs; Scrawl was right.*

Seamus muscled the boat to yet another landing, and Finnegan jumped out, tying the rope to a ring set into the stone. Seamus was next, and he and Finnegan helped Clatter out of the boat. No one helped Josh and his friends, who got off as best they could.

They were marched up a series of stone stairs. These were much steeper and longer than the ones they'd come down, and Josh was breathing heavily when they reached the top. His skin was soaked with sweat, and his shirt clung to him in the clammy, cold air.

They walked through a doorway and found themselves in a dimly lit basement. Tall filing cabinets lined the rust-stained walls. The drawers on many of them were open, and sheets of paper spilled out like entrails. Josh noticed that several of the papers had small black-and-white photographs stapled to them. *Those are patient records,* he noted grimly.

They came to a set of doors. Clatter pulled a handle that protruded from the wall, and machinery in the walls ground to life. The doors opened, revealing an elevator large enough to accommodate them all. As it lurched upward, the elevator shook with the strain.

Josh watched the buttons on the elevator's control panel light up as they passed each floor. At *4* it shuddered to a stop, and the doors opened.

"Watch your step," Clatter said as he got out with a strange jumping motion. Then Josh noticed that the elevator had stopped a good six inches below the level of the floor outside. The floor itself seemed to sag, as if the ancient building had given up.

"This is where the game will begin," Clatter said. He nodded at Finnegan, who produced a key and proceeded to unlock the handcuffs. Josh massaged his wrists, which had been rubbed raw by the metal. He noticed the others doing the same.

"The rules are very simple," Clatter continued. "There are twelve zombies. Find and kill them all within two hours and you go free."

"We didn't agree on a time limit," Josh objected.

"My customers don't have all night," said Clatter. "And neither do you."

"But this place is huge," Charlie said. "There's no way we can cover it in two hours. You know that."

Clatter nodded. "You may well be right," he admitted. "But as you yourself said," he added, looking at Josh, "you *are* the best Torchers I have."

Josh pushed down the urge to rush Clatter.

"Of course, if you do *not* complete the task . . ." Clatter left the sentence unfinished. They all knew what would happen.

"We'll become zombies," Firecracker said. "Yeah, we get it."

Clatter looked at Firecracker with an expression of amusement. "For someone who has never played the game outside of his bedroom, you're remarkably confident," he said.

Firecracker returned the stare. "We're all good at something," he said slowly. "I'm sure one day you'll figure out what your something is."

Josh enjoyed watching the look on Clatter's face change. Firecracker had landed a direct hit. *You might not be the brightest guy,* he thought, *but I'm glad you're on my team.*

"Your torches are through that door over there," Clatter said, his tone decidedly less friendly. "I'm afraid we forgot to pick up communicators for you. You'll have to stay in contact the old-fashioned way.

You must remain here while we return to the control center. Do not enter the room until you hear the command to begin." He removed a watch from one of his pockets. "Who's going to be the team captain?"

Scrawl nodded at Josh. "I guess I am," Josh told Clatter.

Clatter handed him the watch. "When the game begins, this will start to count down the time remaining," he said. "As usual, there are cameras throughout the building. Your progress will be followed with much anticipation."

Clatter, Finnegan, and Seamus returned to the elevator. As the doors began to close, Clatter looked at Josh and smiled. "Good luck," he said. The sound of his laughter followed the elevator as it descended.

"No communicators," Scrawl said. "Great. He wants us to yell so the z's hear us."

"How are we going to find a dozen zombies in this place?" Charlie added. "We could spend an hour on each *floor*."

"We'll have to break up," said Firecracker. "Each of us take a floor or something."

"No," Josh told him as he put the watch on his wrist. "That's what Clatter wants us to do." He spoke quietly, knowing that if Clatter had put cameras in, then he had undoubtedly installed microphones as well.

"Remember what we agreed on—we stick together. All of us get out of here or none of us do."

Scrawl nodded. "Josh is right," he said. "We have to do this as a team."

"All right," said Firecracker. "Then what's our plan?"

"This place is basically a big square," said Scrawl. "Four corridors around a central open area that used to be a garden. It's where the patients went to go outside without being able to escape. I say we do a basic sweep pattern. Start at one corner, go around until we come back to it, then go to the next level. The place was designed so that the stairs alternate position. On floors two and four they're in the southeast corner. On three they're in the northwest. They did that so that nobody could have a straight shot out of here if they ran. We can use the stairs as a starting position."

"Are we all okay with that?" Josh asked.

Charlie and Firecracker nodded.

"I know I said we would all stick together," Josh continued. "But if we all stay on the same floor, maybe it's okay if we sweep in teams of two. That way we can cover the floor twice as quickly. Whichever team gets to the stairs first waits for the other. We've got half an hour for each floor. If the second team doesn't show up by the time thirty minutes is up, the first team—"

"Goes to the next floor," Firecracker interrupted him.

"No," said Josh. "They go find the other team. Remember, we're *all* getting out of here. Now, does anyone else have a watch?"

"I do," Firecracker said.

"Then you go with Scrawl," Josh told him. "Charlie will come with me. We'll alternate partners on each floor."

"Why?" Firecracker asked.

"So we don't get too comfortable," Charlie explained. "It keeps us fresh."

"All right," said Josh. "Now we wait for the signal."

It came five minutes later, just as Josh thought he wouldn't be able to stand the suspense any longer. A screeching sound filled the hallway, followed by Clatter's voice. It was tinny and faint, and Josh had to strain to hear it.

"Time begins now," Clatter said simply, and the air went dead.

"Go!" Josh called out, and ran for the doors.

He burst through them into a small room. Two beds were against the wall, their metal frames rusted and the stained mattresses on them bursting open. Four torches lay on one of the beds.

"Could these be any older?" Scrawl asked as he

picked one up and slung it over his shoulder.

"Another advantage for the other team," Josh joked grimly. He turned his flamethrower and checked the fuel level. It was at half of what it should be.

"Do you know how to use that?" Scrawl asked Firecracker, who was looking at his torch.

"I'm not sure," said Firecracker. "Where do the arrows go again?"

Despite himself, Josh laughed. He'd missed his friend's careless sense of humor. He suspected Firecracker wouldn't be joking once he saw his first zombie up close, but for now his attitude helped ease the tension, at least a little bit.

"Ready?" Josh asked.

"Ready," Charlie said as the other two nodded.

"Let's go find us some zombies," said Josh.

22

The first zombie was waiting for them right outside the door. Because they weren't expecting one so soon, none of them were prepared for it. Charlie, who went first, walked right into it. The zombie, a huge man in a coverall with HOWARD stitched over the pocket, wrapped his arms around her and immediately went for her neck. Charlie didn't even have time to scream.

Scrawl, following behind her, butted the zombie in the face with his torch, causing him to fall back a step or two. It was enough for Charlie to slip out of his grasp, and with a fierce yell she kicked the zombie squarely in the stomach. It doubled over, and she delivered a roundhouse kick to its shoulder. A moment later the zombie was in flames as Scrawl torched it.

"Come on!" Charlie shouted, waving Josh and Firecracker out of the room.

They skirted around the zombie. Josh saw Firecracker stop and stare at the man, who was on all fours crawling slowly toward them. Firecracker wore a confused expression as if he couldn't believe what he was seeing was real. For a moment he even started to go back toward the zombie.

"Firecracker!" Josh yelled. "Move!"

Firecracker tore himself away from the site of the flaming zombie, and the four of them moved down the hallway. "It was alive," Firecracker said as they went. "It had a name. *He* had a name."

"You can't think about it," Josh told him, although he knew this was impossible. How could they *not* think about it, especially now that they knew how the zombies had been made? But they had to try. Josh reminded himself that nobody would want to live that way, and that if he and his friends wanted to get out of there, they had to do what they had to do.

"Here's our starting point," Scrawl said as they reached the end of the corridor. "Josh, you and Charlie go right. Firecracker and I will go left. We'll meet at the stairs. Remember, we've got eleven to go."

They split up. Josh and Charlie walked side by side as they began their search. The fourth floor seemed to be nothing but patient rooms. Every door they passed opened into a room very much like the first one, with two beds and one small window covered by thick bars.

"Where would a z even hide in one of these?" Charlie asked when they were halfway down the hall and hadn't found anything.

"Could be a small one," Josh reminded her. "A kid."

Charlie looked at him. "Even Clatter wouldn't do that," she said. "Would he?"

"I don't know," Josh answered. "Until a few hours ago I wouldn't have believed any of this."

They reached the end of the first hallway without finding anything, and the second hallway seemed to be a mirror image of the first. By the time they'd checked the fourth room on that side, Josh was getting anxious. Where were all the meatbags? He looked at his watch. Ten minutes had passed. They had five left.

"This is like one of those nightmares where you're trying to get out of a place and keep coming back to the same door," Charlie remarked as they approached the next room.

The next second Josh was on the floor and a horribly disfigured face was hovering over his. He recognized it as the woman whose cell he'd looked into in the lab. She gnashed her teeth, flecking him with spit. He noticed that most of her tongue had been chewed off, leaving her with a bloody stump that twitched from side to side as she tried to talk.

Charlie grabbed the woman by the collar and pulled her back. With a ripping sound the woman's dress tore, and Charlie slipped sideways. Josh could smell the woman's breath as she bent closer and closer. It was worse than the smell in the sewers, reeking of blood and decay.

Josh heard footsteps, and suddenly the woman was pulled away from him, her bloody fingertips clawing at him as she was lifted up. He heard Firecracker yell, "Stay down!" and then felt heat on his skin as a stream of fire erupted over him. A gurgling scream filled the air, followed by the horrible stench of burning meat.

Josh rolled over and onto his knees. As he stood, he saw something on the floor and picked it up. It was a name tag, the kind that people wore at meetings or parties when they wanted to identify one another. HELLO, it said. MY NAME IS. Below this someone had printed, in perfectly even letters, ALICE.

"What is that?" Charlie asked as she peered over Josh's shoulder.

"He wants us to know their names," Josh replied. "He's reminding us that they're human." For reasons he couldn't understand, he folded the tag in half and tucked into the pocket of his jeans. "First Howard, and now Alice," he said. "I wonder who's next."

"Did you guys find anything?" Charlie asked Scrawl.

"Just our friend Howard," Scrawl answered. "Is she your only one?"

Josh nodded. "Ten more," he said.

"And three floors," added Charlie. "Why do I think most of those ten won't be on floors three or two?"

"He's saving them for us," Josh agreed. "But we still have to check every floor. He's making sure we don't have much time when we get to the end."

Charlie looked around, scanning the hallway for cameras. "Are you having fun?" she yelled. "Are you getting all this, you sick bastards?"

Josh took her arm. "Come on," he said gently. "Time's up for this floor."

They took the stairs to the third floor in single file, with Josh leading. As they descended, the condition of the walls deteriorated. Huge chunks of plaster were missing, exposing the wood beneath. Broken pipes protruded like bones from the splintered ceiling, and only a few bulbs still emitted any light. What little they did was thin and watery. Josh turned on the light on his flamethrower, but nothing happened. He clicked it half a dozen times to make sure. The others did the

243

same, with no better results.

"Great," Josh said.

As planned, they switched partners, and Firecracker gave Charlie his watch. Josh, now with Firecracker, took the left-hand hallway. Unlike the fourth floor, the third was a mixture of rooms. The first one they came to was an examining room. The floor was cluttered with old instruments, and a tattered eye chart hung on one wall. A discarded hospital gown, stained and torn, lay across the examination table. Other than that, the room was empty.

Another exam room sat next to the first. As Josh swung the door open, a figure turned toward him. It was a man holding something in his hand. The light in the room was burned out, and it was impossible to see exactly what it was, but Josh thought he saw something wet hanging from the end.

He lifted his flamethrower as the zombie shambled toward the door. He waited until he could read the name on the man's tag—RICHARD—and then aimed at his chest. Just before he hit the trigger, Josh realized what the man was carrying was a hand. Veins and tendons dripped from the wrist where it had been broken from the arm, and on one of the fingers was a ring.

He has both of his hands, Josh thought as he stared

at the zombie. *That means that one belongs to some-one else.*

The man dropped the hand, and Josh stared at it. Something about the ring was familiar to him, although he couldn't place it. It looked like the body of a snake coiled around the finger, its head biting its tail to form a circle.

"Get down!"

Firecracker's voice startled Josh. He looked up just in time to see the zombie reaching for him. Instinctively falling to his knees, he covered his head with his hands as Firecracker's flamethrower roared into action. The zombie wheeled back, shrieking.

"Close the door," Firecracker said. "Roast him."

Josh started to do that, then saw the hand again. Trying not to think about it, he reached out and grabbed it, flinging it outside the room. Firecracker cried out in disgust. "What are you doing?"

Josh slammed the door and pressed his back against it as the zombie tried to get out by ramming his body again and again into the door. Josh could feel the heat from the flames passing through the metal, and every time the zombie hit the door, he jolted Josh forward. But slowly the hits became less and less forceful, until finally they stopped completely.

After checking to make sure the zombie was really

dead, Josh turned back to the hand. He'd been staring at it while holding the zombie back but had come no closer to figuring out why the ring triggered something in his brain. He knelt and reached for the hand.

"Don't touch it," Firecracker warned. "It's got blood all over it. You get that in you and you might as well be that guy," he added, gesturing at the closed door. Smoke was seeping out from underneath it and filling the hallway. It burned Josh's eyes.

"I don't have any cuts on me," Josh said as he reached out and pulled the ring from the finger. It came off easily, and he wiped it on his jeans. "I've seen this ring before," he said. "I just can't remember where."

A muffled scream came from somewhere else in the building, interrupting his thoughts. "Charlie?" Firecracker asked.

Josh shook his head. "No." He put the ring in his pocket, and he and Firecracker ran down the hall. Josh completely forgot about checking the rooms until they started to turn the corner into the next corridor. He stopped. "We should go back," he said to Firecracker.

The scream came again, this time louder and more frenzied. Josh looked down the hall just as someone rounded the corner, running straight for them. Whoever it was moved much more quickly than zombies usually did, with a rolling gait that carried the body forward in weird zigzagging steps.

For a moment Josh *was* afraid it was Charlie, but in the dim light it was impossible to tell. Then two more figures came around the corner. He saw flames flickering at the ends of two torches and knew the figures were Charlie and Scrawl. Which meant that the screaming figure was a z.

The zombie kept coming. Then, when it saw Josh and Firecracker standing with flamethrowers pointed at it, it stopped. It started to turn, but Charlie and Scrawl were closing in from the other side. The zombie raised its arms as if to cover its face with its hands, and that's when Josh saw that its right arm ended in a stump.

"On three!" he heard Scrawl shout. "One! Two! Three!"

All four of them fired their weapons at the zombie. It was consumed in a fireball that immediately blackened the walls and ceiling. Flames whipped around the zombie like a tornado. The creature stood perfectly still for a few seconds, then collapsed into a pile like burning leaves. Josh and Firecracker stood on one side of it, looking through the fire at Charlie and Scrawl.

When the flames died down, Charlie ran to Josh.

"She knew," she said. "She *knew* we were going to kill her. I've never seen one run away before." She choked back tears. "Josh, it was horrible."

Josh reached into his pocket and removed the ring. "Have you seen this before?" he asked Charlie.

She took the ring and looked at it. Then her hand began to shake.

"Freya," she whispered. "It's Freya's."

23

"There are eight left," Josh said as they pounded down the stairs to the second floor. He clenched his fist, feeling Freya's ring press against his palm. Rage burned in his chest. He looked at his watch. "Forty-five minutes left," he called out. They had wasted time, and it was his fault. After they torched Freya, he had fallen apart, cursing Clatter and screaming in pain and anger over what his friend had been turned into. The others, not knowing what to do, had let him yell it out.

Now he was filled with new strength. Eight z's stood between him and Clatter, and he was determined to find them. He strode down the hallway, abandoning the two-to-a-side plan and kicking in every door he saw. The second floor held more examination rooms, as well as what seemed to be offices for the doctors. They found the next zombie in one of those, standing by the wall and staring dumbly up at a framed diploma, like he was trying to read it. Josh noted the name on the z's tag—PAUL—before giving Scrawl the okay to torch him.

They found two more zombies on the floor, a woman named Gwen sitting in a kind of living room staring at an old broken television set, and a man named Virgil hiding in a closet. They each went down with barely a fight.

"I've got to say, these meatbags have been pretty tame," Firecracker remarked as they regrouped at the head of the last flight of stairs. "I've played holo-z's meaner than these ones."

"He's saving the worst for last," said Scrawl. "I guarantee it. Probably the ones who've been turned the longest. They're totally gone. Nothing inside but pure instinct to kill."

"Whatever they are, they're still people," Charlie said, shooting Firecracker a dirty look. "Remember that."

"Okay," Josh said. He checked the fuel level on his flamethrower. "We're low on firepower and we've got five more zombies standing between us and walking out of here. I don't know what we're going to find down there, but whatever it is, I'm not going down without a fight."

"I'm with you," Scrawl said.

"Me too," Charlie agreed.

Firecracker nodded. "Let's do it," he said.

"What's our time?" Scrawl asked Josh.

"Twenty-five minutes," Josh answered. "None to waste."

They went down the stairs. The first floor was different from the others. There were no examination rooms, no offices. In fact, it looked like a hotel lobby—one that had been bombed over and over again. The walls were covered with water-stained wallpaper that hung in ribbons where it had fallen away. The dusty old furniture had nearly disintegrated into piles of sawdust and scraps of velvet. A huge chandelier that had once hung in the asylum's grand foyer lay on the marble floor, its shattered crystals sparkling like diamonds in the moonlight that managed to find its way through the boarded-up windows.

"This is the only floor the families ever saw," Scrawl said as he surveyed the ruins. "The administrators wanted them to think this was more like a country club than a mental hospital."

"So where do we go?" Charlie asked.

"That way is blocked," said Josh, looking down the hallway running south. The ceiling there had caved in, and the corridor was impassable. "It looks like we don't have a choice."

"He's herding us," Scrawl said. "Whatever is down this way, Clatter set it up."

Josh nodded in agreement. "Then let's get the show over with," he said.

The hallway seemed to go on forever. They moved quickly, taking turns stepping into any rooms they came to and doing a quick sweep. Josh didn't expect to find any z's there, and they didn't. *He's trying to get us to run our time out*, he thought.

Finally they came to the intersection of the north and west corridors. Like the south corridor, the west was also blocked by debris. The only option remaining was to go through a small door set in the inside wall.

"The garden," Scrawl said. "He wants us in the garden."

Josh tried the handle of the door. It turned easily, and the door swung out. Moonlight flooded the hallway, and Josh blinked a couple of times. After the darkness of the upper floors, even the weak light of the quarter moon took some getting used to.

The walls of Feverfew rose up all around the garden. The dark panes of the windows stared blankly out at the overgrown plants and the crumbling fountain at the garden's center, where headless figures stood reaching their cold hands up to the sky. The air was rich with the smells of dirt and rot.

"They could be anywhere in there," Charlie said, looking at the jungle of trees and flowers. "There's no way we can find them in time."

"Then they need to find us," said Josh.

The others looked at him, confused. "How?" Firecracker asked.

"We torch the whole place," Josh said. "The one thing they're afraid of is fire. We'll smoke them out. There's only one way in and out of here, right?"

"As far as I know," said Scrawl. "But Clatter could have made another one."

"We'll have to risk it," Josh said. "We're almost out of time."

"But how will *we* get out?" asked Charlie.

"One of us will guard the door," Josh said. "Make sure nobody locks it. The other three will set fires." He looked at Charlie. "You stay here."

"Why me?" Charlie argued. "Why not him?" She nodded at Firecracker. "He's the one with no experience."

Firecracker snorted. "What kind of experience do you need to set something on fire?" he countered.

"You're guarding the door *because* you have more experience," Josh said to Charlie. "If anyone—or anything—tries to come through that door or close it, you stop them."

"All right then," Charlie said. "Go start your fires."

The three boys headed for the trees. "We'll start in the back and move this way," Josh said. "Firecracker, you take the left. Scrawl, you take the right. I'll go up the middle. We run through, start blasting, and run back here. Got it?"

"Got it," Scrawl and Firecracker said.

"And don't forget, there are z's in there somewhere. Don't engage them, even if you see them. You'll just get stuck in the crossfire. Avoid them and get back here."

Scrawl looked at him. "You think this will work?"

"I don't know," Josh answered truthfully.

He counted down from three. At one, the three of them took off into the garden. Josh saw Firecracker and Scrawl disappear into the darkness; then he was plunging headlong through the overgrown grass. It was still wet from the rain, and he hoped it would light.

He drove that thought from his mind as he pushed past some wizened bushes. Then he was running through a patch of rosebushes. Their thorns snagged in his clothes and scraped his hands, but he ignored the pain. He could see the far wall of the garden twenty yards ahead of him. As it grew closer, he lifted his thrower.

A flash erupted from his right. Scrawl had reached the wall. *He always was the fastest of us,* Josh thought as he came to a stop and aimed the flamethrower at a clump of dead weeds. As he fired, a third blast came from the left. Firecracker had made it too.

The fire took hold, snaking up the stalks of grass and hungrily consuming it. It seemed to hesitate for a moment, then jumped to a nearby tree. The dead wood popped and exploded as the flames wrapped around the desiccated limbs. Josh watched long enough to make sure the fire wasn't going out, then turned and started running back to the door.

When he reached the fountain at the center of the garden, he bore left to go around it. As he did, a zombie leaped out of the muck that filled the basin and flung itself at Josh. It was covered in slime, and its hands grasped at Josh's arm but slipped away. The zombie fell, its fingers catching hold of Josh's leg. Josh stumbled, tried to wrench loose from the zombie's grip, and went down hard on his back. The air was knocked out of him.

The zombie awkwardly got to its feet and came at him. Josh scrambled for his flamethrower, but he had fallen on top of it and couldn't get it. He had nothing to defend himself with. *This is it,* he thought. *I lost.*

A figure charged out of the darkness to his left,

bellowing madly. The zombie, confused, stopped its forward rush. Then Josh saw Firecracker aim his flamethrower at the thing's head and fire. The zombie crackled as the flame made contact with the water soaking its skin and clothes. Steam exploded off its head, enveloping it in a black shroud of smoke and steam.

Firecracker pulled Josh to his feet. "Nice work," Josh said, grinning.

The two of them ran as fast as they could back to the doorway, where Scrawl and Charlie were standing with their throwers at the ready. "What happened?" Scrawl asked. "You guys were right behind me."

"We had a visitor," said Josh. "But we took care of it."

"You mean *I* took care of it," Firecracker corrected him.

"Just look for z's," said Josh. "They've got to be coming out sooner or later."

As if on cue, four zombies emerged from the smoke. They walked slowly and heavily. One, already on fire, clawed at its charred shirt. The other three headed for the four friends and the door.

"Four of them and four of us," Charlie said. "Pick your z, boys."

The four of them fanned out, each one heading

for a different zombie. Scrawl took the one that was already smoking, hitting it dead on with a blast that peeled the skin from its torso. Charlie took on a massive man who, even after being set afire, continued to walk toward her until a second blast from Scrawl took out the zombie's legs and left it a pile of melting fat.

Josh advanced on his target. To his left Firecracker was toasting his zombie, which left just one to go. For the first time Josh allowed himself to think that they really might get out alive.

Then he saw the zombie's face. "Stash," he whispered.

Stash saw him and stopped. His dead eyes stared at Josh, and his mouth began to move. His head rolled from side to side as well, and his arms twitched spasmodically. Josh raised his flamethrower. But as he took aim, he saw Stash's mouth move again. Something about it wasn't right. He wasn't just making random sounds. *He's trying to talk,* Josh realized.

Before he knew it, he was running toward his old teammate. He heard Charlie, Scrawl, and Firecracker screaming for him to stop, but he kept going, coming to a halt only when he was just out of Stash's reach. Stash turned his head, looking at Josh, and mumbled. Josh still couldn't hear him.

You have to get closer, he told himself.

Fighting every one of his natural instincts, he took another step toward Stash. Stash didn't move. Josh took another step, then another, until he was right in front of Stash. He looked into the boy's one remaining eye. It was milky, and thick yellow ooze dripped from the corners. But then, just for a moment, it seemed to clear, and Josh almost believed he was looking at the old Stash.

"Home," Stash mumbled. He pressed something into Josh's hand. Then, before Josh knew what he was doing, Stash staggered back, pretending to be hit, and fell into the flames that had engulfed the garden. Josh watched, a scream stuck in his throat, as Stash disappeared behind the wall of fire.

The next thing he knew he was being pulled back by Scrawl and Charlie. "We have to get out of here," Charlie yelled above the roar of the inferno.

Josh turned his back on the garden and followed his friends through the door. When they were in the hallway again, Firecracker shut the door behind them. "Now what?" he said. "We got them all, didn't we?"

Scrawl nodded. "Yeah," he said. "But somehow I don't think we're done yet."

"What are you holding?" Charlie asked Josh.

Josh looked at the key in his hand. "Stash gave it to me just now. But I don't know what it's for."

Scrawl took the key from Josh and looked at it for a long moment. "I think I know what this is," he said.

"What?" asked Josh.

"You know how Clatter wears that coat with all the keys sewn on it?" Scrawl said. "He doesn't just do it because it looks cool. He does it to hide things." He held the key up. "Things like this."

"What's the key to?" said Firecracker.

Scrawl held the key up. "If we're lucky—the way out."

24

"**C**latter is a genius," Scrawl said as they walked. "But he's also paranoid. He has escape routes all over the place. I think this key opens the door to one of them."

"How do you know?" Charlie asked.

"Here," said Scrawl, pointing to one end of the key, where the letter *F* was stamped. "F for Feverfew." He turned the key over, and on the other side was the number 237. "Room 237," he said. "Whatever this key unlocks, it's in that room."

"What if it isn't?" asked Firecracker. "What if Clatter gave him the key to trick us?"

Josh thought about the look in Stash's eye when he handed over the key. A lump formed in his throat. "I don't think he did," he said.

"Okay," said Firecracker doubtfully. "Then let's get up to room 237 and see what's up there."

They headed for the stairs, but the ding of the old elevator drew their attention. The doors opened, and Clatter emerged with Seamus and Finnegan. He strode across the lobby toward where the four exhausted friends stood.

"Play along," Scrawl whispered to the others as Clatter got closer.

"I must say, you've impressed me," Clatter said. The tone of his voice was warm, but Josh heard an undercurrent of frostiness that he didn't like. "Your methods on the final test were a bit crude, but given the time constraints, rather brilliant."

"I'm glad you liked it," Scrawl said. "Now how about keeping your end of the deal?"

Clatter took a deep breath. "As much as I'd like to, I'm afraid I can't," he said. "You see, you didn't complete the game in the allotted time. You were exactly one minute and seventeen seconds over."

Scrawl shook his head. "I knew you'd never let us go," he said.

"Mmm," Clatter replied. "Your lack of faith in me is disappointing. But it's irrelevant, as you lost."

"So now what?" said Josh. "You kill us?"

Clatter feigned shock. "Of course not," he said. "They do." He nodded toward the stairs, where a dozen or more zombies were shambling toward the lobby.

"And now I will say good-bye," said Clatter. He, Seamus, and Finnegan walked rapidly toward the waiting elevator, stepping inside. As the doors shut, Clatter tipped his hat and smiled. "Good luck!" he called out.

Scrawl glanced at the zombies, then ran for the elevator. "Help me!" he yelled to the others.

Josh, Charlie, and Firecracker joined him at the doors. Scrawl looked up at the needle over the door. It was only halfway between the lobby and the basement. He shoved the grate that covered the elevator doors aside and started prying them open.

"What are you doing?" Josh said. "We have to get to the second floor."

"We can't let them get out of here," said Scrawl, trying to force his fingers into the crack between the doors. "If we don't stop him, Clatter will keep on doing what he's been doing. He'll just replace us with other players. More people will die."

"And how are we going to stop him?" Charlie asked.

"There's a hand brake on top of the elevator," Scrawl said. "The mechanics used them for stopping the car during shaft maintenance, when they rode on the roof to access the pulleys. If I can get to it, I can stop the car between floors and trap them there. That way the police will know just where to find them."

"There's no time for that," Firecracker said.

"Not if you keep arguing," said Scrawl. "Now help me get these doors open."

Firecracker and Josh took one door while Scrawl and Charlie took the other. At first the doors wouldn't budge, but then they reluctantly creaked open. Josh peered inside. He could just see the top of the elevator car.

"We'll wait for you upstairs," Josh told him. "In room 237."

Scrawl shook his head. "Don't wait," he said. "In case something goes wrong, I want you on the way to the police. Now get out of here."

Josh started to object, but Scrawl was already lowering himself into the shaft. He clung to the ladder. "Go!" he yelled. "Now!"

Josh and the others turned and faced the zombies. In order to get to the stairs, they were going to have to fight their way through, and they had no weapons left. Even then, they had no idea what waited for them in room 237. *It could be nothing,* Josh thought. *We could be walking right into a trap.* But it was their only chance.

"We can't kill them," Josh said. "So let's just get through them. Don't let them grab you, or you'll probably get bit."

"Really?" Firecracker said. "Thanks for the tip." He grinned at Josh. "Race you to the second floor," he said, and took off.

Josh watched as his friend ran straight at one of the zombies at the front of the pack, a fat man wearing a blood-spattered butcher's apron. Firecracker lowered his shoulder and hit the z square in the chest, sending him flying backward into some of the other zombies. They fell like bowling pins, and Firecracker shouted, "Strike!" triumphantly.

Charlie and Josh followed him, dodging the zombies that grasped clumsily at their clothes. Firecracker was already halfway up the first flight of stairs, calling for them to hurry. Charlie ducked under the arms of a zombie woman swinging her purse like a weapon—and Josh, who was behind her, was hit right in the face by it. He fell backward, hitting his head on the tile floor.

Stunned, he couldn't move. He saw the zombie woman's face as she leaned over him. Her milky eyes rolled back in her head and her mouth opened, revealing broken teeth. She dropped her purse and reached for him with hands covered in sores.

"Back off, meatbag!" he heard Charlie yell.

The zombie woman turned her head, snarling, as Charlie's foot hit her in the stomach. The z let out a grunt and was flung to the side. Then Charlie was grabbing Josh's hand and pulling him to his feet. His head throbbed as he stood, and for a moment he thought he might faint.

"Come on!" Charlie encouraged him. "We're almost there."

Josh forced himself to move. He saw the stairs ahead of them, clear of z's. They just had to get to the second floor. His feet moved up the steps as behind them the zombies moaned in frustration. Josh knew they would follow, and even though they moved slowly, there were a lot more of them.

As they reached the landing, a body fell in front of them, almost hitting them. The zombie—a teenage boy—twitched frantically, trying to move his broken limbs.

"Sorry!" Firecracker yelled, looking at them over the balcony. "I didn't know you were there."

Charlie and Josh stepped over the z and ran up the rest of the stairs. Josh's head still hurt, but it was clearing. When they met up with Firecracker in the second-floor hallway, he looked at the number on the nearest door.

"Room 237 is this way," Firecracker said, pointing to the left. "And we should probably hurry. Company's coming."

Josh and Charlie turned and saw four zombies coming up the stairs, moving with surprising quickness. The three friends dashed down the hall, finding the room about halfway down. They'd passed the room during their sweep of the floor, but because it was locked, they had assumed it was zombie free. Digging the key from his pocket, Josh jabbed it into the keyhole and turned it. For a moment nothing happened, and Josh's stomach sank. The four z's were getting closer.

Then there was a click and the lock slid open. Firecracker and Charlie slipped into the room, with Josh entering last. He slammed the door shut and turned the lock just as a zombie face appeared in the window, pressing its bloody mouth against the glass.

Josh turned away from it and surveyed the room. They didn't have much time. The z's would either break the glass or break the door down. Whatever was in the room Josh and the others had to find it, and soon.

But the room was empty. Completely empty. There wasn't a chair, a desk, a bed—not even any trash.

"What is this?" Firecracker said. He turned and looked at Josh. "I told you this was a trap. Now we're stuck in here, and sooner or later those things are going to get in." He pointed at the door, where the faces of two more zombies were peering in at them. They were also banging on the door, and it shook in its frame.

"Not so fast," said Charlie. "There's a closet."

"Oh, a closet," said Firecracker. "That makes *everything* better. We can just hide in there until the meatbags go away."

Ignoring him, Charlie went to the door in the wall and turned the knob. She pulled the door open, stepping back in case there were any surprises inside. When nothing jumped out, she looked in.

"What is it?" Josh asked.

Charlie shook her head. "I'm not sure," she answered.

"Well you'd better figure it out in the next thirty seconds," said Firecracker. "That door isn't going to hold."

There was pounding on the door, followed by the sound of breaking glass. Outside, the zombies' moans grew more frantic. "Like I said," Firecracker yelped, pushing Charlie into the closet as he grabbed Josh by the wrist and pulled him inside too.

There was barely room for the three of them in the closet. Not that it really mattered. As far as Josh could tell, they were simply inside an ordinary closet, an *empty* ordinary closet. There were no weapons in it, not even coat hangers. The only thing in there was a single old-fashioned lightbulb hanging from the ceiling.

The sound of breaking glass came again, and Josh peered out to see a zombie reaching through the window of the room's door and grabbing its doorknob from the inside. Soon the room would be filled with z's, and there would be no escaping them this time. There were too many of them, and without weapons Josh and his friends would be zombie food.

Acting on instinct, Josh pulled the closet door shut as the first zombie staggered into the room. Now the closet was pitch black. Josh could hear himself breathing heavily as he thought frantically for some way out.

"I'm not dying in the dark," Firecracker said, reaching up and pulling the frayed string attached to the lightbulb.

The light flickered on. A second later the floor fell away beneath them. Josh, Charlie, and Firecracker shouted in surprise as they plunged into darkness. Above them the light continued to burn but grew smaller and smaller as they fell.

A few seconds later, Josh landed with a thud on something soft. Charlie fell next to him, and Firecracker landed on top of them both. He rolled off with a grunt and sat up.

"Where are we?" he asked.

Josh looked around. They were on top of what

seemed to be a pile of old mattresses—at least six or seven of them—in some kind of cellar. The mattress they were sitting on was stained, and it stank of mold and dirt. It sagged beneath their weight, and Josh had to roll to the left to get to the side and throw his legs over the side.

That's when he saw the old ambulance. Large and white, it had a fat, round fender over each wheel and a long front end with circular glass headlamps that looked like eyes. A single red light stuck up from the roof. On the side door was painted a big red cross, and underneath that, in black, the words FEVERFEW ASYLUM.

Firecracker jumped down from the mattress and looked at the ambulance. "This thing must be at least a hundred years old," he said.

Josh climbed down from the mattress pile and helped Charlie down as well. Once on the ground, Charlie eyed the ambulance doubtfully. "*This* is the big secret of room 237?" she said.

Firecracker, who had gone around to the other side of the ambulance, called out, "The keys are still in it!" Then the door beside Josh and Charlie opened. "Get in!" Firecracker ordered.

Josh looked at Charlie. "He's got to be kidding."

Before Charlie could answer, something fell onto

the mattresses behind them. Josh turned and saw a zombie flailing around, trying to turn itself over. A second later another one fell from the hole in the ceiling, and then another.

Charlie looked at the ambulance, then at Josh. "I don't think we have a choice."

She and Josh climbed into the ambulance just as one of the zombies managed to roll off the mattresses. It lay on the floor for a moment, then moaned and got up. It turned its head toward the ambulance, where Josh was looking at it through the window.

"Can't you get this thing started?" Josh asked as the z snarled and spat out strings of bloody drool.

Firecracker was turning the key in the ignition. The engine made choking sounds but didn't start. More zombies had fallen to the floor, and now, attracted to the sound, they started congregating around the truck. There were half a dozen of them. They stared in the windows with milky yellow eyes, their faces only inches from the glass. Josh looked away.

"I don't know what to do," Firecracker said, his voice cracking. "This thing is ancient."

"The clutch!" Charlie yelled. "Push in the clutch!"

Firecracker looked at her in bewilderment. "The what?"

Charlie pointed to one of the pedals near the floor.

"You have to push that in and put the gears into neutral, otherwise you can't start the engine."

Firecracker pushed tentatively against one of the pedals with his foot. "This?" he said.

"Switch seats," Charlie ordered, climbing over him.

Firecracker scooted next to Josh. "How do *you* know how to drive this thing?" he asked as Charlie fiddled with the pedals and pulled on the gearshift that rose up from the floor.

"My father has an old Mustang," she said. "It was *his* father's, and someday it will be mine. He taught me how to drive it when I was twelve." She turned the key, and the engine sputtered. A zombie banged on the passenger-side window, which cracked.

"Go!" Josh said as the zombie hit the glass again. "Go, go, go, go, go!"

Charlie turned the key again. This time the engine rattled to life. The zombies began to bang on the ambulance, roaring angrily. The one outside Josh's window hit the glass once more and it shattered, the pieces falling all over Josh's lap. A rotting hand came through the opening, reaching for Josh's hair. He smelled the stench of decomposing flesh.

Suddenly the ambulance leaped forward, knocking a z to the ground. There was a sickening crunch as the tires ran over it. Charlie pulled on the gearshift, and the ambulance shuddered. Something inside made a grinding sound. But a moment later they were moving ahead even more quickly.

"Where are we going?" Firecracker asked as Charlie drove down what seemed to be a long corridor cut through solid stone.

"The only way we *can* go," said Charlie. "Unless you want to go back and ask for directions."

Charlie turned something on the dashboard and the headlights came on, producing two thin beams of weak yellow light that barely cut through the darkness. They could see a little way ahead, but not far enough to see the two wide doors that barred the end of the corridor. By the time they loomed into view the ambulance was headed straight for them.

"Hang on!" Charlie yelled as she urged the car forward.

A second later they hit the door. Wood splintered, one of the headlights went out, and the ambulance shook, but it didn't stop. Instead they found themselves emerging onto a road. Josh leaned out the window and looked behind them. On a bluff above them Feverfew loomed in the darkness.

"That must be how they took patients in without anyone seeing them," he said, glancing at the mouth of the tunnel they had just exited. He shuddered as he thought about the possibility of the zombies getting out through it. *We'll get to the police before they can*, he reassured himself. *They'll come block it up again*.

Charlie steered the ambulance down the narrow, twisting road that led away from the hospital. Unused for decades, the road was falling apart. Pieces of it were gone, and in other places plants grew up from cracks in the pavement. As they bounced along over bumps and ruts, Josh prayed that the old ambulance would stay together.

"If I'm right, this road connects to the Upside Highway," Charlie said. "We can take that to the police station at Citytop. That's the closest one."

"Are you kidding?" said Firecracker. "It will take forever to get through that traffic."

Charlie scanned the dashboard, pushing and pulling on knobs. The windshield wipers went on, then off. The remaining headlight blinked out and came on again.

"What are you looking for?" Firecracker asked.

A shrieking sound pierced the night, and a red light lit up the dark around the ambulance. "That's what I'm looking for," Charlie said as the siren wailed.

As she had guessed, the road did lead onto the Upside Highway. And everyone did get out of the ambulance's way. Now that they were away from Feverfew, and Clatter, and the zombies, Josh allowed himself to think about Scrawl. Was he okay? Had he trapped Clatter, Seamus, and Finnegan and gotten himself out? Josh hoped so. *He's a smart guy,* he reminded himself. *He'll be fine.*

He also thought about his family. He knew they were worrying about him. He couldn't wait to call and let them know he was okay. Even more, he couldn't wait to see them again. The first thing he was going to do was apologize to his parents for ever thinking the game was harmless fun. The second thing he was going to do was tell Emily what a great sister she was. He hadn't allowed himself to think about it during the game, but now that it was all over he realized how close he'd come to never seeing them again.

Suddenly the tiredness that had been growing all night began to overtake him. He leaned back and closed his eyes. *Maybe it's all a bad dream,* he thought. *Maybe I'll wake up in my own bed.*

He dozed for a few minutes, until the jerking of the ambulance coming to a stop woke him. "We're here," Charlie said.

When they walked into Precinct Number 42, Josh felt safe for the first time since leaving his house that afternoon. They were in a police station. They would tell someone their story, Clatter would be arrested, and they could go home. Someone else could worry about the zombies roaming around Feverfew. His career as a Torcher was over.

As they walked to the front desk, they were surrounded by a sudden flurry of excitement. Uniformed policemen ran past, paying no attention to them. There was frantic talking, and the buzzing of com units filled the air as invisible voices shouted directions.

"What's going on?" Charlie said. "Where are they going?"

Josh turned around to see what was happening. Outside, dozens of police vehicles were starting to pull out of the station lot, their lights spinning. Then he noticed the screen above the door to the building. It was tuned to a local news channel, and although Josh couldn't hear what the reporter was saying, he saw the word *zombies* scroll by on the news ticker running below the picture.

He, Charlie, and Firecracker looked at one another. "No!" Josh said.

He looked back at the screen. This time he saw the whole headline: ZOMBIES SIGHTED IN OLD TOWN. GET TO SAFETY. MORE INFORMATION TO FOLLOW. The picture showed a street in Old Town. Half a dozen zombies were lurching down the street. The camera zoomed in on one of them.

Charlie gasped. Then she sobbed. "It can't be," she said. "Josh, no. It's not—"

"It's Scrawl," Josh said.

A man approached the zombies. He was wearing a black uniform with a familiar logo on it. He pointed his flamethrower at Scrawl.

"No!" Firecracker shouted.

As fire burst from the flamethrower, Charlie buried her head in Josh's neck and sobbed. He held her close, telling her that everything would be all right.

But it won't be, he thought. *It will never be all right again.*

MICHAEL THOMAS FORD

is the author of the teen novel SUICIDE NOTES as well as several essay collections and adult novels, including JANE BITES BACK. He lives in San Francisco with his partner and their five dogs. Visit him online at www.michaelthomasford.com.